THE SEVENTH DEVIL

Suzanne Craig-Whytock

Copyright © 2021 by Suzanne Craig-Whytock

All rights reserved. No part of this publication may be reproduced or transmitted in any form or by any means, electronic or mechanical, including photocopying, recording or any information storage and retrieval, without the written permission of the publisher. Names, characters, places and incidents are either the product of the author's imagination or used fictitiously, and any resemblance to actual persons living or dead, events or locales is entirely coincidental. All trademarks are properties of their respective owners.

Published by
BookLand Press Inc.
15 Allstate Parkway
Suite 600
Markham, Ontario L3R 5B4
www.booklandpress.com

Printed in Canada

Library and Archives Canada Cataloguing in Publication

Title: The seventh devil / Suzanne Craig-Whytock.
Names: Craig-Whytock, Suzanne, author.
Identifiers: Canadiana (print) 20210156856 | Canadiana (ebook) 20210156872 | ISBN 9781772311433 (softcover) | ISBN 9781772311440 (EPUB)
Classification: LCC PS8605.R3467 S48 2021 | DDC C813/.6 – dc23

We acknowledge the support of the Government of Canada through the Canada Book Fund and the support of the Ontario Arts Council, an agency of the Government of Ontario. We also acknowledge the support of the Canada Council for the Arts.

For Ken and Katelyn

*There's the devil you know and the devil you don't,
the devil you'll meet and the devil you won't,
a devil that's tall and a devil that's small,
and a devil that's human after all.*

Have things gone awry in your life?
Are you haunted by the past?
Are your personal demons getting the best of you?
Then contact DarkWinter Direct at darkwinterdirect@mail.com.
Reasonable prices. Discretion guaranteed.

1

TERENCE KENT

The driveway was pitted and uneven, worn smooth in spots where the gravel had long since washed away. The pickup truck bounced and recoiled from the potholes, the fifth wheel trailer we were pulling behind us grinding and wrenching against the hitch. I grabbed the armrest to stop from being shaken out of my seat. Gareth breathed in sharply, irritated at the gross negligence that he was obviously assigning to the owner of the driveway and the non-descript house at the end of it. We shuddered finally to a halt and sat for a moment, observing. The radio was on low, playing some oldies station from Sault St. Marie that Gareth kept tuned to for white noise. He snapped the radio off abruptly and put the truck windows down to listen; hot, humid air infiltrated the air-conditioned cab. There was no sound from outside, not even a bird chirping or a cicada.

"Well," he said brusquely. He was flexing his fingers on the steering wheel, gripping it tightly, then releasing it. Grip, release. Grip, release.

We sat in the silence for another minute. I sighed nervously. "Okay, then."

We opened our doors and got out of the truck, walking around to meet at the middle of the front fender. Gareth leaned back against the hood and spat into the dirt. "I predict," he said, "that this one isn't going to be any fun."

"They rarely are," I answered, staring at the house. There was no sign of movement inside, at least not yet, and the silence was like being in a vacuum, which wasn't unusual under the circumstances. We moved forward together, and one of the curtains danced slightly as if someone had brushed against it. The house was plain, a white vinyl box with nothing to recommend it. The sidewalk leading to the front door was full of cracks—I instinctively avoided them, the childhood rhyme whispering in my ear: "Step on a crack, break your mother's back." It was tempting, but I stepped over them all the same. The whole place had an air of surrender to it—the flower beds were choked with weeds, the lawn was overgrown, and the roof had at least a dozen shingles missing. There were several rose bushes at the side of the house that looked almost dead, the leaves and the petals of the blooms brown and brittle.

The front door swung inwards slowly; the whining creak it made was the first sound we'd heard so far that hadn't come from either of us. There was a figure silhouetted in the doorway, then the silhouette became a man as he stepped out into the light. He was thirty, maybe more—it was hard to tell. Balding, face worn, eyes bleary and red-rimmed, shoulders slightly stooped as if he'd been carrying something heavy for a long time. Terence Kent.

"You're here," he said, in a voice hoarse from disuse.

Gareth looked up and examined the clouds above us, his hands in his pockets. He wasn't much of a people person. I said, "Yes. Would you like to invite us in?"

The man blinked against the sun, silent for several heartbeats. Then he exhaled slowly and whispered, "Come in then." He sounded almost angry. We followed him into a dim hallway lined with jackets that hung from hooks on the walls, stacks of takeout pizza boxes, and garbage, a claustrophobic tunnel. The air was acrid with the smell of old smoke, and another, sweeter scent beneath it. Gareth's nose twitched and wrinkled with distaste. I realized why the odor of burning was so strong as we moved further into the recesses of the house. There was a tiny kitchen with space enough for a table and two chairs below a window that was broken out. A highchair stood in the corner. The back wall of the room was damaged, blackened where a fire had scorched the wallpaper and burned through the ceiling, creating a hole. The imprint of the flames continued up into the next storey.

The man led us into a stuffy living room. He pulled a pillow and blanket off the well-used couch and gestured for us to sit. It seemed pretty apparent that he'd been sleeping on it right before we arrived—the cushions were still warm. There was an old recliner in the corner, green tweed. A woman sat in it, her arms crossed defiantly. I ignored her for now. Gareth stayed standing, his gray eyes moving, examining things in his own way. I knew that he was more sensitive when it came to scents so I let him take the lead.

Gareth sniffed the air again. "You've had a fire here, that's obvious. But there's something else—it smells like—"

"Roses," the man interrupted.

"Yes," Gareth agreed calmly, taking a seat next to me on the couch. The man suddenly disappeared, then reappeared carrying a chair from the kitchen. He put it down next to the television and sat on the very edge, planting his feet in front of him and leaning slightly forward.

"How—how much?" It was the first thing they always asked. And the answer was always based on how much they looked like they could afford. This was the part that Gareth left up to me. Talk of money made him uncomfortable and he stared down at his hands, flexing them again in his lap.

"Five hundred for the first hour, Mr. Kent. Then we'll see after that. It depends on how difficult it turns out to be."

Terence Kent massaged his temples with the thumb and middle finger of his right hand, then looked square at me. "Okay."

"Good," I nodded firmly. "We already know a little from your email, but tell us about your…problem in a bit more detail."

He sniffed and rubbed his eyes with the heels of his palms, rocking slightly back and forth on the edge of the chair. "It's—it's Naomi." His voice was choked with emotion. The woman in the corner snorted derisively and rolled her eyes. "We got married about two years ago. We met in town at the bar. I was 32 and she was 24—not a huge age difference, and I thought we'd be fine. But once we moved in here, she got… restless. Hated being alone during the day when I went to work. She started going out at night, back to the bar, not coming home until all hours, then the day drinking started. I think she was an alcoholic when we met—I just didn't realize it."

"Bullshit!" the woman in the corner hissed. "You made me this way."

"Then," he carried on, "she got pregnant. Everything changed. The drinking stopped, she got a part-time job at the grocery store, planted flowers, spruced the place up. The rosebushes out back? She planted those the day she found out about the baby—Naomi and roses. There are bottles of rosewater on the dresser upstairs and the house just reeks of the stuff. I've cleaned the place from top to bottom, even steamed the carpets but I can't get rid of it. Anyway, I really thought things were better. But I was wrong. When little Isla was about 3 months old, Naomi said she wanted to go back to work. I said no, we couldn't afford a sitter, and what was the point? I made enough for both of us, but she said, 'I'm bored. I didn't sign up to be some brat's nursemaid for the rest of my life.' I left it for a while, hoping she'd grow to love Isla, but that didn't happen. What *did* happen is that she started drinking again. Then about three weeks ago, I was at work when I got the call." His voice broke and he wrapped his arms around himself, rocking back and forth more noticeably.

We waited patiently. This was always the hard part, talking about what happened. I breathed in and out evenly, aware that the woman in the corner was staring hard at me but choosing not to engage her yet. Gareth sat still, unblinking, as he always did—I'd never met anyone who could remain motionless for so long. Finally, Terence Kent shuddered and looked at us. "There was a fire. While I was at work. She was drunk—she lit a candle on the kitchen table. A rose-scented candle. The fire department said the wind must have blown the curtains into the flame and they caught. They went up in a flash. She didn't notice because she was passed out in that chair there."

He gestured at the chair in the corner and the woman sitting in it leaned forward, arms still crossed. "Screw you, Terence!" she hissed at him.

He continued. "If the neighbours hadn't seen the smoke, the whole place would have burned down. As it was—" His voice caught, and he choked back a sob. "Now, I can't leave the house. Every time I try, a fire breaks out. I'm trapped here. I just want to leave, go somewhere else and get away from the memories—and the smell."

"All right," Gareth said, standing up abruptly. "I need to go out to the truck and get the equipment. Why don't you come with me, let Verity get prepared?"

Terence Kent sniffed, his face full of misery. "Do you want the money now or after?"

"After is fine," I answered gently. He followed Gareth out, and I sat back against the worn couch cushions. "OK, Naomi, I think it's time for you and me to—"

"I'm not going in the box!" she declared adamantly, pressing herself into the chair as if that would prevent the inevitable.

"Well, you can't stay here," I responded, staying calm. "You know that."

"Yes, I can! And he deserves it, after everything that happened. He lied to me! He told me that he had money, and then he brought me *here*. Look at this place! He never wanted to do anything, go anywhere. And then I had to go and get pregnant."

I was used to the fury, to the excuses. "It doesn't matter," I said simply. "You have to leave."

She continued on, oblivious. "The baby wasn't even his! It was Landon's. He told me to sit tight, that he'd come get me, but he didn't. He just ditched me like they always do. I was so *angry* that day…."

Gareth came back into the room alone. He was carrying a duffel bag in one hand and a small rosewood box with a hinged lid in the other. The box looked ancient and had symbols carved into it. Naomi stared at it in horror and pressed her lips tight together. Gareth put the bag down on the floor and held up the box. "She's here?"

I gestured subtly towards the chair in the corner.

"I don't see anything from the baby."

I nodded my head. "Already gone on."

"Well, that's something." He bent over and opened the bag, pulling out a glass jar of salt which he placed on the coffee table. At the sight of it, Naomi jumped to her feet. The room was suddenly filled with the sickly-sweet scent of roses. "I'm not GOING!!" she screamed, taking a step towards us. The chair in the corner started to smoke and then burst into flames.

I hated fire. I jumped up from the couch and yelled, exasperated, "Enough! We can do this the easy way or the hard way. But if we do it the hard way, you never get to see Marl again."

Naomi's eyes widened and she hesitated. Flames were crawling up the wallpaper, charring it, and the room was starting to get heavy with smoke. Gareth and I wouldn't be able to breathe easily much longer.

"What are you talking about?" she demanded.

"Marl. He's waiting," I said softly.

Gareth gave a slight cough, and I continued, trying not to sound worried. "Terence said you were always Marl's favourite, that he took you fishing, and looked after you when your mother was working. He says your favourite memory is the day you and Marl planted rose bushes together in his garden, that it made you so happy."

The flames suddenly extinguished and the smoke began to clear. Naomi looked as if she was about to cry. "My grandfather is there?" she whispered.

"Of course," I said. "Where else would he be? Get in the box, Naomi. He's waiting for you."

She laughed and said skeptically, "That's really the box? It's way too small. How am I supposed to get in *there*?"

Gareth held it out in front of him and lifted the lid. "The box is just a symbol. Once you decide to go in, everything will fit just right."

"Marl was the only one who ever cared about me," she said, tears spilling over her soot-covered cheeks. "You promise he's there?"

"I promise."

She stepped forward. "Don't tell Terence I set fire to the kitchen," she said sadly. "He really loved Isla. Better that he believes it was an accident."

She went to put her hand inside the box, but I suddenly clutched Gareth's arm and pulled it back. "Just one thing," I said, trying to keep the hope and desperation out of my voice. "Is there anyone nearby here named Harmony? She'd be around six years old." I held my breath waiting for her answer, but Naomi just shook her head.

"Sorry. The only other one like me is an old guy who curses in Italian all the time. No Harmony." I exhaled slowly and signalled to Gareth, who held the box back out. She put her hand in it and then she disappeared. The scent of roses began to dissipate until there was nothing left but the faint lingering smell of smoke.

I slumped down onto the couch, exhausted and deeply disappointed. The old familiar grief came flooding back. Gareth sat down next to me, the box on his lap, leaned back and put his feet up on the coffee table. "I know," he said.

"I know you do," I answered.

Terence popped his head around the corner of the door. "Is it…is she…?"

"Yeah," Gareth said. He sat forward, grabbed the jar of salt and put it back in the duffel bag. "Glad we didn't have to use that."

"What's it for?" Terence asked, coming into the room fully. He looked relieved, like they sometimes did. Other times, they cried—or laughed.

"We'll take the money now," Gareth said, ignoring the question. He put the box into the duffel bag as well, zipped it up, and hoisted it over his shoulder.

Terence stared at him for a second, then said, "Oh—right!" He disappeared again, this time reappearing with a fistful of crumpled tens and twenties. "Here you go. She… she won't come back, will she?"

"No," I said flatly, heaving myself up off the couch. "She won't."

2

GARETH

I met Gareth on my nineteenth birthday. I'd been on my own for a few weeks, living rough in an ancient, battered Ford Tempo that I'd 'borrowed' from my parents; apparently, they hadn't cared enough to report it because I'd had more than one cop knock on the window and then leave me alone when I said I was just taking a nap before getting on my way.

I'd been driving from town to town, parking the Tempo on a side street then finding a busy corner where I could set up and play my guitar for a while before I got chased off. It wasn't panhandling, it was busking—let's be very clear about that. I'm not a beggar. And people could be really generous, especially on a sunny day, so I made enough to eat and pay for gas. But it was getting harder—I'd been having moments of wretched despair, and they were getting worse as time went on.

On my nineteenth birthday, I was almost done with the whole thing. My chest was hollow, and breathing felt like one step away from breaking. I'd been playing in a place called Kincardine, a cottage town on the lake where people had money for a girl who knew some Dylan and The Hip, and a few originals; before long, my guitar case was glinting with coins and even rustling with a couple of bills. It was dusk, and I was packing up when a guy approached me. He was non-descript—a face like everyone and a tan jacket—but something about him made me feel ill at ease.

"One more song? C'mon." Then he smiled. It was the smile of a vulture, looking for bones to pick.

"Nah," I answered, carefully casual, snapping shut the latches on the case and picking it up. I turned to leave, but he reached out as if to put his hand on my arm and I felt a glimmer of something. I moved away and shrugged the feeling off. "Hey. I'm meeting someone. Over there." I pointed up the street towards a place called Milly's, a type of roadhouse with loud music and light spilling out onto the pavement. He didn't look convinced and stared at me hard with eyes that suddenly flashed yellow as the streetlights snapped on, so I added, "It's my birthday—there's a party waiting." Party of one, but he didn't need to know that.

I strode away purposefully, listening intently to make sure there were no clicking footsteps following close behind. One quick glance back—he was still standing there, watching, so I had no choice. I ducked into the doorway of the bar and went through. I was immediately enveloped by warmth. There was a raucous group of people sitting at a table in the back, and their laughter was comforting. The place was decorated in 'roadhouse chic'—pub tables and wooden chairs, chalkboards advertising the specials, and a long bar. Up at the front by the bar, one stool was occupied. Over in the corner, at a table for four, a woman sat, stringy blonde hair hanging in her face, her impressive chest straining against the cheap polyester shirt she was wearing.

I sat down at the bar at the far end, away from both her and the occupant of the other stool, an older man whose face was hidden in the shadows of his drink. I stared straight ahead, trying to avoid looking at the woman, who was reflected in the mirror behind the bar, until the bartender came over and said, "I'm gonna need to see your ID."

I handed my driver's license over wordlessly, the picture on it a younger version of me, solemn and unsmiling. "Hey! It's your birthday! Congrats—whaddaya want?" he exclaimed cheerfully, a counterpoint to my own feelings about the occasion. I'd never been in an actual bar before; my previous drinking experience was tossing back tequila in the sugarbush behind Eric Shah's house. The bartender passed me a drinks list, and I peered at it blankly.

"I don't know. What do you recommend?"

He thought for a second and laughed, "A lot of ladies like the Blue Hawaiian, but you look more like a Zombie girl."

"Fine. Make me one of the walking dead," I answered solemnly. He didn't realize I was more serious than he thought.

The drink hit me hard. I hadn't eaten much all day, and after about three sips, the room was suddenly in sharp relief. After half a glass, I was feeling looser. And when I tossed back the last ounce, I caught the eye of the woman in the corner. I swivelled around on my bar stool and addressed her. "What the hell are you looking at?" She continued watching me and sniffed, rubbing the back of her hand under her nose. Her hair dripped water onto the table. I was suddenly filled with fury and yelled, "Leave me alone!"

The bartender appeared quickly. "Hey! What's going on?"

I turned to him, my eyes blazing, then realized that the stool next to me was now occupied by the man who'd been at the other end of the bar. "She's fine," he said. "Glass of water." The bartender went over to the sink at the back. "Calm down," the man said.

"Calm down?! *You* calm down. You don't know what I can see," I hissed at him.

"Yeah," he replied. "I get it."

"Are you making fun of me?" I demanded, slurring slightly. "Do you think I'm crazy?'" I remember slamming my hand down on the bar for emphasis. The bartender turned and my companion held up his drink and said, "Get me another one of these while you're there." The bartender gave a thumbs up and walked away.

"Nope," the man said. "I'm not, and I don't."

"She won't stop staring at me," I whispered.

"Yep," the man said.

"Don't humour me, you asshole." I raised the empty glass to my lips, trying to taste the last few drops.

"Her hair smells like the lake. Sometimes she cries." He accepted the glass of water and his fresh drink from the bartender, who looked at us suspiciously but left us alone now that I seemed quiet.

"Her name is Kelli. With an 'i'," I continued.

"Ah," he replied, taking a long swallow and then putting the glass down carefully and deliberately on the bar. "She tell you that or are you psychic too?"

"It's on her name badge. She's wearing some kind of uniform. Can't you see it?"

"Nope."

I looked at him hard for the first time. He was thin, all angles and sharp edges, and tall, judging by the way his knees almost touched the bar even though his feet were on the bottom rung of the barstool. His hair was steel gray, cut short and neat, and his eyes were the same steel gray, framed by black glasses. He appeared to be about fifty, but I was never great with age—he could have been older or younger than that, but I knew one thing. He was old inside, like he'd seen too much, understood too much about the world to not be weary of it. I knew how he felt.

"How do you know she's there if you can't see her?"

I asked him, trying not to make eye contact with her in the mirror, worried about what might happen if I did.

"There's a shimmer," he said. "And then there's the smell." He wrinkled his nose and picked up his glass again.

I sniffed the air. "I don't smell anything," I said.

"And I don't see anything. Just the shimmer. Like tiny sparks in an empty place." He caught the bartender's attention and gestured for another. Then he called out, "Make it two." The bartender furrowed his brow, but he waved him off. "She's okay—I'll vouch for her."

The bartender shrugged and poured out the shots. I accepted mine with a smile to let him know that I'd found some equilibrium. "I'm Verity. Verity Darkwood," I said.

"Gareth Winter." He stared into his drink as if the answers to all the questions in the universe were contained within it. Then he said, "What should we do now?"

I was taken aback. I would never have guessed this was where the situation was going; I thought the drink was because he felt sorry for me. But when I asked harshly, "What do you mean?", he laughed, and I realized that I'd misread his intentions.

"Nothing like that," he said, still laughing and shaking his head. "I meant, about *her*. Do you want to talk to her—"

"I never talk to them!" I whispered sharply.

His eyebrows arched up in surprise. "You should. You'd be amazed at what they can tell you." He paused. "I would imagine." The laughter from the group of people in the back suddenly grew louder and filled my ears. Below the laughter was something darker, ominous, a kind of low, animalistic growling that floated just underneath. I spun around on the barstool. The woman at the table, Kelli, had turned to look as well, her eyes wide with fear.

"Do you hear that?" I asked Gareth in a quiet voice.

He nodded. "I think it's coming from him." He gestured with his chin almost imperceptibly towards someone at the back. It was the man from the street, non-descript, tan jacket. He was standing in the corner, in the shadows behind the loud group who didn't seem to notice him. His face was shrouded in darkness, except for his eyes, which flashed yellow as they moved from watching the group to looking over at us.

"I think we should leave," I said, turning to Gareth. "I met him outside before. There's something wrong about him."

Gareth leaned over sideways and reached down into a duffel bag that was sitting on the floor beneath his bar stool. His arms were so long that he didn't even need to get off the stool. He pulled out a jar of what looked like salt and put it very slowly and deliberately on the bar in plain sight. "It's all right," he said wryly, tossing back what was left of his drink. "Nothing to worry about."

I picked up the jar to examine it, but when I put it back on the bar and glanced over my shoulder at the man in the corner, he was lost in the shadows again. A burst of laughter erupted from the large group, but this time it was just laughter, nothing more. Kelli relaxed and went back to staring in the mirror and sniffing.

Gareth returned the jar to his duffel bag and stood up. "Come on," he said. "Let's go." He pointed to the table where Kelli sat sniffing and dripping. I didn't want to follow him, but the alcohol made me bold. Or reckless. She didn't say anything when we sat down, just looked at us wide-eyed.

"Uh…hi," I said haltingly. I had no idea what the point of this was, but Gareth's eyes were bright with anticipation. Kelli said nothing, just kept on staring. I was at a loss. I always thought they must be so lonely, that if I talked to one of them, they'd be eager to answer. "Why…why are you here?" I asked. "Did you used to work here or—"

Kelli's mouth opened with a choking sound, and water suddenly poured out, gushing down her chin and onto the table, creating rank pools that crept towards the edge and trickled onto the floor. I jumped back in shock, but Gareth, who could only see the water, stayed composed. He swirled his finger in it, then held his finger to his nose. "Lake Huron," he pronounced with barely restrained excitement. It was the only time I've ever seen him like that in the years since. "Ask her," he said. "Ask her what happened."

How do you describe a conversation like that? The water belching out of her in between the words, the strange, bloody tears, the anguish and grief, the complete and dizzying disorientation of finding herself back in the place where she had met the man who killed her instead of in the better place she was promised. "I just stopped in for a quick drink after work. He seemed nice. We went for a walk on the beach but then..."

Finally, Gareth was satisfied. He reached into the duffel bag again and pulled out a small, carved wooden box with a hinged lid. At the sight of it, her face lit up with joy, and she sobbed in relief. I had no idea what was going on. He held it in front of himself, opened the lid, and said, "It's time." She nodded.

He looked at me for direction. "She's ready," I said, but for what, I wasn't sure. He held the box up towards her.

"Wait!" I called out, struck by a sudden thought. "Do you know anyone named Harmony?" She shook her head, barely acknowledging me, fixated on the box. She reached out towards it and put her hand into it. Then suddenly, she was gone.

Gareth closed the lid gently, almost reverently and asked, "Did it work?"

"Did *what* work?" I asked back, watching him carefully. He was looking at the box in wonderment, turning it around to gaze at it from all sides.

"It was only a theory," he said, almost to himself. Then he quickly put the box back into the bag and called for the bartender.

"What do you guys need—hey! Did you spill something over here?!" The bartender looked confused, and Gareth and I burst out laughing, the kind of nervous laughter you make after something strange has happened.

"Give us a couple more shots," Gareth said. "And a towel. We'll clean up."

It was actually more than a couple of shots, and then everything became a blur. I woke up the next morning in the back of a fifth-wheel trailer, fully clothed, head pounding, mouth full of cotton but it was the first time in a long time that I'd slept straight through until dawn. Gareth had slept in the cab of the pick-up that the trailer was hitched to. When he came in, neither of us said anything for a while. He made some coffee, and we sat in silence, drinking it while the sun made its way up the curtains. I was thinking about the night before and what it all meant. Finally, he spoke the words that I'd been dreading to hear. "Tell me about Harmony," he said.

3

HARMONY

Yes
Yes
Yes
No
What are you going on about now, Verity?
Some of the houses are good and some of them are bad.
Stop talking nonsense.

The houses — I always knew. We would be out driving and sometimes I had to look away because after a string of 'Yes' houses, buildings that were perfectly normal and kind, there would be a 'No', a house that breathed danger or evil, a house where something bad had happened, or might yet happen. I thought everyone was able to see it, and couldn't understand why anyone would want to live in one of the bad houses, but as I got older, I realized it *was* just me. I tried to explain it to my mother, but she wouldn't hear it. And for a long time, I half-believed she was right, that it was childish nonsense and that there was something wrong with me, until I was 14 and we were taking what dad liked to call "the scenic route" on a summer trip to visit relatives in Leamington. We drove through a small town called Merlin, and as we passed a house on the main street, I felt something reach out for me, something dark trying to suck me in. I gasped, pressed myself hard into the upholstery of the Ford's back seat, and squeezed my eyes shut tight. Harmony, who was about six at the time, reached over and poked me.

"What's wrong, Veevee?" That was what she always called me. When she was first learning to talk, she couldn't say 'Verity'. I didn't mind — she was the only person who called me Veevee and it made me feel special in her eyes.

"I don't like that house. It's one of the bad ones," I whispered back. Harmony swivelled in her booster seat to look out the back window.

"I don't see it."

"We're past it now," I answered, relaxing a little. Then my mother jerked her head around. She had that look, the one that let me know how much she really didn't like me.

"Jesus, Verity, what the hell is wrong with you? Stop scaring your sister! We've talked about this before — you're too old for that bullshit. Michael, pull the car over!"

My father, who said very little under normal circumstances, did what he always did — he obeyed immediately without a word. The car slid over to the curb and my mother jumped out. She yanked open the back door and demanded, "Get out of the car. We're going to finish this once and for all. We're going to knock on the door, go in, and then you'll see how ridiculous you are!"

"No, I—" I started to say but she interrupted me.

"Get out of the damn car!" She grabbed my arm and started pulling while I struggled to pop my seatbelt. My mother was a big woman, much taller than me when I was fourteen, with strong hands and a very moody nature. I knew there was no point in arguing with her when she was having one of her meltdowns. Harmony's eyes were welling up with tears — she really did look scared now.

"It's okay," I whispered. "I'll be right back." My father, as usual, said nothing.

"Which house is it that you're so afraid of? Point to it!" my mother ordered. I did, reluctantly, and she proceeded to drag me by the arm down the street until we were standing in front of it. It was a plain house, brick, with windows like dead eyes. I stiffened and she was just about to start up again, when we heard a voice call out from behind us.

"Can I help you with something?" An elderly man stood on the curb across the street. He was about 75 years old, white hair, carrying a cane. He walked towards us, leaning on the cane and limping slightly.

"No," my mother answered brusquely. "We're fine."

"Well, if you want to take a picture, you better hurry up. The owners don't like looky-loos hanging around."

I wasn't really paying attention, more concerned with the sharp mouth of the metal screen door, but my mother stared at him hard. "What are you talking about? Why would we want a picture?"

"Oh, sorry," he said, gesturing at the house with his cane. "I thought maybe you were part of the fan club, you know, for the Chambermaid Murders. Can't believe after all this time people still want to see the house where it happened."

My mother blanched and loosened her grip on my arm. I wasn't really paying too much attention; I was fixated by the way the house seemed to breathe out foul air that spoke of terrible spaces inside, of harsh light, bare mattresses, chains, garbage, and death. My mother's voice finally broke through: "Verity! I said come on!" and it shook me out of the nightmare. I looked at the old man blankly. Suddenly he grinned and his face changed from kindly to fiendish.

"He stabbed her and then beat her to death," he whispered. His voice sounded thick and wet, like he was gargling blood, and his eyes flashed yellow. "Why don't you go in and see?"

I stifled the scream that was building in my throat, and turned to watch my mother, who was storming down the sidewalk towards the car. When I looked at the old man again, he seemed bewildered but normal. "You—you have a nice day," he said, his voice shaking a little. Then he turned and limped back across the street. I walked to the car quickly, got in, and buckled my seatbelt, not saying a word to anyone. My mother just stared straight ahead in silence as well. Dad sighed, a put-upon sound that hurt me more than he could ever know. Harmony reached out her tiny hand and placed it on top of my mine. I smiled at her weakly and she smiled back, a little gap-toothed smile that I still dream about.

That fall, she disappeared.

It was my fault. Even if I hadn't been told that by my mother over and over again, there was no denying it. It was my fault.

We'd started going to different schools that year. Harmony was in grade 1 at Bellwood Public School, and for the previous two years, we'd taken the bus together while I was in middle school and she was in junior and then senior kindergarten. She loved the bus; she would jump up and down with excitement every morning when she saw it trundling down our street, her blonde hair already sneaking loose from the ponytail I'd put it in. On the way home, we would play a game called "What did you learn today?" and she would screw up her face, thinking hard, until she came up with something like "If you mix red paint and blue paint together, it makes purple!" or "3 apples and 1 more is 4 apples."

The local high school was a ten-minute walk in the other direction, so we didn't ride the bus together anymore. Still, it was my job to see Harmony safely off in the morning and to be there at the end of the day to meet her. The bus stop was near a busy intersection and my mother was worried that she'd wander into traffic or go the wrong way and get lost. I didn't mind—my classes ended a good hour before her school let out, which gave me plenty of time to walk to the bus stop. But that day there were soccer try-outs after school. I loved soccer, and I wanted to be on the team so badly, to do something just for me, and maybe make a couple of friends. And if I hadn't been so selfish, Harmony would still be here. See, I miscalculated. I thought I'd have enough time to suit up, try out, and then get to the bus stop right before the bus arrived. But there were a lot of girls and the try-outs ran late, and then I was racing down the sidewalk, knowing that the bus had dropped her off at least five minutes ago, thinking what if she was scared, what if she *did* wander off, and I was running so hard that my heart was coming out of my chest. And when I got to the corner, she wasn't there.

I stayed calm for the first ten minutes. I figured that she had probably gone home on her own, so I ran to the house, hoping desperately that I would find her sitting on the stoop, waiting for me. When I couldn't find her at home, I took off back the way I'd come, towards the town and the shops by the corner where she'd been left, furious with the bus driver for letting her off alone, and convinced she must have gone into one of the stores. I kept checking my phone—she had my number written in permanent marker on the inside of her backpack—and I was expecting a call from someone at any second telling me that she had come into their store or knocked on their door, lost and scared, but that she was being taken care of until I got there.

The phone call never came.

Finally, I had no choice—I called my mother at work. When I admitted to her that I was late to the bus stop and now I couldn't find Harmony, she lost her shit, screamed at me to go home, that she would call the police, and that if anything had happened to Harmony...the threat hung in the air, vague and terrifying.

The rest of that first evening was a nightmare. The police came and interviewed me, my parents staring daggers at me. They started a search immediately and put out an alert on social media. Then things got even worse when the officers came back. There were two of them, a tall, heavy-set man called Egler, and his partner, a dour-faced woman that he called Bentley. He asked the questions while she took notes:

Egler: So, Verity. You claim that you last saw your sister this morning, is that right?

Suspect: Yes, when I put her on the bus.

Egler: And you're absolutely sure about that?

Suspect: Of course! Why are you asking me this?!

Egler: We spoke to the bus driver —

Suspect: Did he explain why he let her off the bus all by herself? She's only six!

Egler: Well, here's the problem. He says he didn't let her off by herself. He says that you were there waiting for her like you always do. He even described you, right down to the Toronto FC soccer jersey you're wearing right now. Says the two of you were bouncing a rubber ball back and forth.

Suspect: No! I was late to the bus stop. He must have... imagined it or something! I haven't seen her since this morning. (Suspect begins to cry)

Egler: How would you describe your relationship with your sister?

How would I describe my relationship with Harmony? I loved her, plain and simple. She was the only thing tethering me to any kind of life that mattered. I knew my parents didn't care about me particularly; they both treated me as if I was some terrible obligation that had been thrust upon them too soon. But Harmony...she was a beautiful little dream of a child. My mother doted on her and even my father would suspend his self-imposed isolation from the family to take "his girl" on an ice-cream date or to the school fair. You'd think I would have been jealous but I wasn't.

For some reason no one could figure out, and which baffled and often infuriated my mother, I was Harmony's favourite person. From the moment she could first say my name, it was "Veevee" all the time. Her face lit up when I came in the room, and as she got older, it was "Veevee, come!", her order to go and play some game of her own invention. When she woke up in the night from a bad dream, it was me she cried out for, me she wanted to cuddle her until she fell back asleep. So the thought that the police could even *consider* that I had somehow harmed her was devastating to me. Even after the bus driver grudgingly conceded that he *might* have been mistaken, even after a security camera from one of the stores showed me tearing down the street at exactly the time I'd said, my parents still looked at me with suspicion, distrust, and a considerable amount of hatred.

The police investigation went on for months. At first, it was intense; the security camera that proved my innocence also showed a beige car, almost out of the frame, licence plate obscured, parked in the same spot for hours and then taking off just before I ran past. All the media outlets were showing it, imploring the driver to come forward and tell the police if they'd seen Harmony, or anything suspicious. Then the attention shifted—could anyone who recognized the car or driver, or had seen a little blonde girl near the car please come forward? The clip of the car sitting there and then suddenly leaving was posted on the internet by our local news station. I watched it over and over, hoping to see something the police hadn't, a shadow on the sidewalk, a reflection, anything at all. I locked myself in my room and cried until I was dehydrated and sick, obsessed with that beige car. They searched all the woods in the area, put out national bulletins, plastered every hydro pole and store window with her pixie face. But no one ever came forward and Harmony was never seen again. And it was all my fault.

4

MR. WIGGLES

"I hate cats," Gareth said flatly.

We were climbing up the stairs in an older apartment building in Regina. The elevator was broken and we were on the third-floor landing with three more flights to go. The stairwell was dimly lit and smelled of a combination of cooking, musty clothes, and urine.

"So you've told me," I said, stopping to catch my breath. "Several times. I've never had one. My parents didn't like animals. I don't know how I feel about cats."

"You'll find out soon enough," he said, sniffing the air. "They reek something terrible too."

We reached the sixth floor and stepped through the stairwell door out into the hall. It was stuffy and humid; the old wallpaper was peeling away at the edges and corners, and the carpeting was stained—small, discoloured circles that led towards number 6.

"Follow the yellow brick road," Gareth intoned dourly. He was wearing a peaked cap that echoed the sharp angle of his chin and cast a shadow over his eyes. He took it off for a moment, ran his fingers through his hair, then put it back on firmly. "Ready?"

I nodded. He dropped his duffel bag onto the soiled carpet and knocked on the door. The knock seemed to echo for a second, and then in the vacuum of silence that followed, we could hear the sound of meowing. It was quiet at first, then it rapidly turned into a crescendo of mewling and yowling. Suddenly, the door opened and a very large woman flew out and slammed it behind her. The draft of air she produced was heavy with ammonia—cat pee, to be specific—a more intense version of the smell in the stairwell. She was unkempt, wearing a stained housedress, and faded slippers. I couldn't help but notice that there was some kind of gravel on the carpet where she stood, as if she had dragged cat litter with her on her soles.

"You're here," she breathed out, her voice full of relief. "Thank the good Lord."

"Thank your email, Ms. Murillo," Gareth responded cynically. The email in question had arrived in the darkwinterdirect inbox two days prior, a somewhat hysterical and poorly written missive about an "unnatural" feline infestation. I was intrigued, Gareth was resistant, but we both agreed that we needed the money *and* the diversion. We were crossing the Prairies anyway, and I know Gareth was as bored as I was of the never-ending flat landscape, so it didn't take much to convince him, despite his dislike of the furry, four-footed creatures.

The woman stared at him, confused, with large brown eyes, and I interjected. "You said you needed help with your...cats?"

"They're not cats!" she whispered fearfully. "Well, some of them are—but not *all* of them! They're terrorizing me!" Her bosom heaved and she placed a hand delicately on it, the way a Southern belle would. The gesture was a sharp contrast to both her appearance and surroundings, and I felt a sudden twinge of sympathy for her.

"Why don't you tell us what the problem is, Ms. Murillo," I suggested gently.

She looked at me gratefully and began. "Please, call me Brenda. I take in strays. The neighbours don't like it—" She paused as Gareth snorted in sympathy with the neighbours. She gave him an angry glare. "I don't care! I can't stand to see an animal suffering. But two weeks ago… or was it three? I've lost all track of time with this nightmare! Anyway, I was out shopping for cat food, and I saw a poor little thing in the alleyway, a scruffy tabby with a bent tail. He looked like he'd been on his own for a while, all skinny and dirty, so I gathered him up to take him home, you know, to feed him and clean him. And that's when the trouble started with the others."

"Others?" I asked. "How many cats do you have?" The yowling coming from inside the apartment made it seem like there were dozens, but that wasn't likely.

"Well, I had thirteen," she said, "but after I rescued Mr. Wiggles, the others showed up too. Now, there are twenty of them."

"What do you mean, 'showed up'?" Gareth asked. "You mean in the neighbourhood?"

"No!" she exclaimed. "That's what's so awful. I can't leave the apartment—every time I try to go out, another one runs in! It's like they're waiting!"

"But we didn't see anything when we got here—" I started, but Brenda put her finger to her lips and gestured silently towards the end of the hallway where it continued around the corner. Gareth and I looked, just in time to see the shadow of something ducking back, and the padding of small feet moving away.

"There's one down there," she hissed. "Waiting. Anyway, it wasn't long after I brought Mr. Wiggles in that the cats started to act strange."

"How can you tell?" Gareth asked snarkily. "Cats are always strange."

Brenda gave him a hurt look, and I glared at him. "Brenda, tell us what happened."

The story, in a nutshell, was that somehow, Mr. Wiggles got control over the other cats. They started off initially by sitting in formation, staring at her while she watched TV. If she went to the kitchen, they would circle around her, Mr. Wiggles watching as if he was orchestrating everything. Other cats began showing up until she was afraid to open the door. Then Mr. Wiggles started to talk.

"I'm not crazy!" Brenda protested.

"We know," Gareth said. "What did it—he say?"

"He said, 'Brenda, don't you think it's about time you changed out of that horrifying housedress and went to the store? We're absolutely famished.' Then he bared his teeth and hissed at me. His voice sounded like an old-time actor, you know, with an English accent. I had to look up 'famished'—it means 'starving'." Her eyes began to fill with tears. "That proves I'm not crazy, right? I didn't even know what he meant. And I don't know anyone English!"

"I think it's time we go inside and meet Mr. Wiggles," I said. "You might want to stay out here."

Brenda protested—when we knocked, she'd been staring through the peephole, on the lookout for the next terrible tabby or cunning calico, and she would rather stand guard inside the apartment than outside of it. She gave a quick, nervous glance toward the bend at the end of the hallway where a shadow paced and waited, its tiny paws making a dull, muffled sound on the stained rug.

"No," she said, shaking her head violently. "I don't want to. I'll stay next to the door, but *inside*, not out here."

Gareth gave his silent assent by hoisting the duffel bag onto his shoulder. I agreed as well. The shadow around the corner was making me uneasy; the whispery sound of tiny feet patrolling the hallway was amplifying in my ears, becoming more of a strange squelching, sticky sound, as if the carpet was soaked with something. I didn't want to think about what it might be.

"We'll need to be fast," Gareth said quietly. "Everyone ready? On the count of three."

When Gareth reached three, he shoved open the door quickly and we all rushed inside. Brenda went first, pushing herself up against the wall in her small foyer. I followed—as I passed Gareth, I could see movement from the end of the hall, something small and shapeless streaking towards us. Then Gareth was in as well, slamming the door against whatever was coming.

We all just stared at each other in silence, breathing hard. Brenda's face was pale; beads of sweat had broken out on her forehead even though the apartment was cool. From beyond the foyer, the chorus of mewling and intermittent yowls increased in intensity.

"All right, Brenda" I said. "Don't come any further into the apartment. No matter what you hear. Okay?"

Brenda nodded vigorously as Gareth and I ventured from the foyer into the small apartment. The main living area was both a sitting room and kitchenette. There were two doors leading from the main room—presumably, the bedroom and bathroom. These doors were closed. The room Gareth and I were standing in was sparsely furnished; there was a worn sofa upholstered in what was once a bright chintz pattern with a matching armchair and footstool, a lamp table, and a TV stand. The end wall contained a bank of cupboards with a sink, stove, and refrigerator. There was a small table with two chairs tucked into the corner. It would have been a normal apartment for a single woman, except for the row of brightly-coloured plastic litter boxes that lined the space between the kitchen table and the sofa. There must have been ten of them at least, which accounted for the overpowering smell of cat urine.

As we entered the room, the mewling escalated. The cacophony was coming from the twenty cats which were perched in pairs or small groups on every possible surface in the small room, lounging on the couch, on top of the television, sharing leftovers on the kitchen table, leaning down to peer at us from the top of the refrigerator. The only exception was the armchair, where a single cat sat silently, staring at us.

It was a large orange tabby, unremarkable in every way except for a slightly bent tail and the inscrutable look on its face. "Mr. Wiggles?" I asked. Abruptly, the meowing and yowling stopped as if a switch had been thrown, and thirty-eight other eyes were upon us, waiting in hushed anticipation. I suddenly remembered that a group of cats was called a 'glaring' and I understood why.

The cat that Brenda called 'Mr. Wiggles' continued to observe us in the silence that ensued. After a moment, he yawned, a wide yawn that exposed sharp, yellowing teeth and a rough pink tongue. Then he spoke. He said, "Who exactly are *you*?"

Brenda was right. He *did* sound like an old-time British actor; in fact, he sounded almost exactly like James Mason. His voice was bemused, and I could have sworn he raised an eyebrow, if cats actually had eyebrows.

"Malevolents disguised as cats," Gareth whispered to me in disgust. 'Malevolent' was Gareth's catch-all term for any evil force that could manifest itself in another form. Every culture and religion had them—they just went by different names depending on whose mythology they belonged to.

Mr. Wiggles turned his attention to Gareth. "Why not?" he asked. "It's as good a form as any. Except, of course, for the containers full of gravel. Appalling." He waved a paw imperiously towards the row of litter boxes.

Gareth breathed in sharply through his mouth, his sense of smell overwhelmed by the aroma of ammonia in the air. As for me, I was simultaneously fascinated and horrified by Mr. Wiggles, who seemed to radiate ennui and enmity at the same time.

"Regardless of the form, you can't stay here, Mr. Wiggles," I told him.

He regarded me with disdain. "Of course I can. Brenda is most accommodating and I have my friends. I see no reason to pull up stakes, so to speak. I'm quite content to remain."

Gareth dropped his duffel bag on the carpet and the cat looked at it out of the corner of his eye with a flicker of suspicion. "Oh, put that away," he continued. "Your tricks won't work on me." Gareth bent down and unzipped the bag. "Put it away!" the cat roared. The rest of the cats yowled in protest as if echoing Mr. Wiggles' ire.

Gareth smirked to himself and pulled out the jar of salt. "Mr. Wiggles," he scoffed.

"That's just what the idiot woman calls me," the cat replied, his eyes flashing yellow. "Do you not know me?! I am Malphas the Profane!"

"Malphas the Pussy, more like." Gareth shook the jar of salt at the cat, who hissed and clambered up onto the back of the chair. The other cats fell silent and stared. Six of them came down from their various perches and advanced on us until we were encircled by them.

"You have no power here," Malphas proclaimed, his ears twitching with uncertainty. Gareth ignored him and unscrewed the lid of the jar. The six cats in the circle began hissing and pacing. Gareth reached into the jar, and in one swift movement, he pulled out a handful of salt and flung it in a wide arc. Malphas screeched and leapt out of the way behind the chair, but the other six weren't as nimble. The salt hit them and the air was filled with a sizzling sound as they began to—well, the best way I could describe it is to say they started deflating, as if they were furry balloons that someone had just popped. As they grew flatter and flatter, hundreds of legs sprang from their sides until they resembled house centipedes. Their tiny little legs in motion, they began frantically racing around the room. I jumped back, shuddering involuntarily with revulsion. Gareth tried to stomp on one as it scurried by—it swerved suddenly, avoiding his boot, and headed for the underside of the couch, followed by the others. They all disappeared into the darkness beneath the couch and the room fell silent again.

"All right, Malphas—your turn," Gareth called out. "You can hide but you can't run."

A low rumbling noise filled the room, and from behind the armchair a shadow grew. At first, it looked like a cat, then it stretched and elongated and the creature it belonged to stood up. It was red, pulsing and formless, with yellow eyes. The only part of it remaining that looked remotely like the former Mr. Wiggles was its mouth, stretched into a wide, toothy grin.

"So this is what a malevolent looks like in its true form?" I asked Gareth quietly. He shook his head and the creature answered for him.

"You wouldn't be able to look at me in my true form," he laughed dangerously. "Your ridiculously inadequate eyes can't see in that dimension. Now I advise you to back away. You might have been able to defeat my minions, but I, Malphas the Profane, am more powerful than they."

"You need to get out of here," I said. "Go back to whatever dimension you came from and leave Brenda alone."

"No!! Brenda is mine!" it roared. "Your weapon is useless against me!" The creature seemed to grow taller and began looming towards us. I stepped back, but Gareth held his ground.

"Do you really think the jar is the only weapon I have?" Gareth tutted and shook his head slowly. "This isn't my first rodeo, you know." He bent over, reached down into the duffel bag, and pulled out a small vial. The creature reared back.

"Stop!" it screamed. "All right, hunter. You win this time—best hope we never meet again. But I should warn you. He is aware of you. And the girl. You have not gone unnoticed and there will soon come a time when he tires of you." With that, the creature gave one more expansive pulse, then seemed to collapse in on itself until the only thing that remained was the Cheshire Cat-like grin. Then it too snapped out of existence, and there was nothing left but silence. The thirteen remaining cats seemed indifferent to what had just happened—they were either asleep or vigorously grooming themselves. Gareth strode over to the couch and shoved it away from the wall. Beneath it were the remains of the 'minions'—desiccated and flattened, their hundreds of little legs shrivelled up against their bodies. He kicked them into a pile with the toe of his boot.

I looked around for a garbage bag, but couldn't find one. "Brenda!" I called. "You can come in now. We're just tidying up. Do you have any trash bags?"

Brenda appeared in the doorway of the foyer. Her eyes widened when she saw the pile of husks on the floor, but she hustled over to the kitchen area and opened a drawer. "I have a couple of plastic grocery bags," she called out. "Will they do?" Gareth nodded. She grabbed a broom that was standing in the corner and brought it with her too. Gareth bent down and swept the husks into the bag. As he was doing that, we heard a faint meowing coming from behind the chair. Brenda took a step towards it but Gareth put his arm out to stop her.

"Verity," he said, gesturing towards the chair. I approached it cautiously, peeking around the back. My brow furrowed when I saw a large orange tabby lying there, blinking sleepily at me. It meowed again then stood up, stretched, and walked into the room.

"Mr. Wiggles!" Brenda exclaimed, rushing over and gathering the tabby into her arms. He rubbed his head against her chin and started purring loudly. "How come he didn't end up like—like the other ones?" she asked, her eyes welling up with tears. "Poor things."

"Malevolents inhabit. Minions imitate," Gareth said simply.

Brenda wrote us a cheque for $400, fifty dollars for each minion, and another hundred for getting whatever it was out of Mr. Wiggles. We left her there, still holding Mr. Wiggles, who seemed quite content to be smothered by her affections. Outside the apartment door on the carpet was one last desiccated husk, belonging to whatever had been skulking around the corner. I poked it carefully with the toe of my sneaker but it disintegrated, leaving a dusty stain.

"What did Malphas mean by 'hunter'?" I asked. "And who is 'he'?"

"I'm not sure," Gareth answered. "I need to think. But first, I need a drink to knock that smell out of my nose. Cats."

I nodded and we went to look for a bar.

5

PAPER GIRL

"Look at this!" the woman standing in front of us exclaimed, waving a folded piece of paper at us. She was in her forties, thin, blonde, and full of suburban angst. Gareth's brow furrowed—he was perplexed by her seeming inability to stand still and calmly explain what the problem was. On the contrary, she just kept stalking from one side of the well-appointed living room to the other. "How much more of this am I supposed to take?!" she demanded.

"Can—can you—*excuse me*!" I called out forcefully. That got her attention, and she whirled around to face me. "What exactly *is* it?"

We were in Vancouver. The email bringing us here had been sent to the DarkWinter Direct inbox while we were in the middle of the Prairies at a campground outside of Regina, recovering from our encounter with the meowing malevolent. I'd read it out loud to Gareth, yelling to him through the screen door of the trailer. "It says, 'I'm having a problem with paper. I don't know what to do.'"

Gareth was cooking dinner outside on the grill, and he called back in through the door, "Wouldn't hurt to check it out. Might be nice to go to the coast." He brought in a plate of burgers and started setting the table while I composed a response: "Please forward address. We will arrive on Friday at 4 pm. If we are delayed, we will let you know in advance."

The trip out to British Columbia was uneventful though, and we did arrive on Friday as promised. One of the advantages of being an insomniac was that I could drive the night shift if I had to, so we made good time. I didn't mind not sleeping; I'd gotten used to functioning on about 4 hours a night. When I did close my eyes, all I could see was Harmony, the way she looked the last time I saw her. She was wearing pink leggings and a long pink T-shirt with a unicorn made out of sequins on it. Above the unicorn, it said, "Powered by sparkles and glitter." I'd put her hair into a high ponytail. She'd lost another tooth the week before, and when she smiled up at me, the tip of her first adult tooth was visible, starting to poke through her gums. I remember thinking, "It won't be long before she's too old for the Tooth Fairy." When she got on the bus, she sat down next to her best friend Harleen, then leaned over her to wave to me from the window. That was the last thing I saw—her little hand waving as the bus turned the corner. And then she disappeared forever. So yeah, it was better not to sleep.

The house we were currently standing in was one of those new monster homes that took up most of the lot, leaving a postage stamp-sized front yard and hardly any room at all between it and the smaller, older houses on either side. The owner, and author of the email, Susan Talbot, was waiting for us at the door, and she was obviously beside herself.

"*It?!*" she cried. "Look at it!" She thrust the paper towards us. Gareth put his duffel back down on the Persian rug and took it from her. He held it up to the light, turning it from one side to the other.

"It's an origami…frog," he said. He passed it to me; I examined it, confirming it was a frog. It was intricately folded and seemed to be made out of a bank statement.

"I *know* what it is!" the woman exclaimed in irritation, still walking back and forth across the living room. "How can I stop it?"

"All right, Ms. Talbot," I said, "why don't you start at the beginning, give us a little background so that we can make sense of all this?"

She stopped pacing, sighed heavily, and threw herself down melodramatically onto a luxuriously deep sofa. "Fine," she said, rolling her eyes at the heavens. "The beginning. My husband and I bought this property about a year and a half ago. There was an older place here, from the '30s, pretty run-down, but we *love* the area, all the revitalization that's going on. So we did what a lot of people in the neighbourhood have done—we demolished the existing house and rebuilt this place. The construction was finally finished a couple of months ago, and we moved in. This was supposed to be our dream home and instead it's become a nightmare!" A tear threatened to spill from the corner of her eye, and she dabbed it away delicately. She sniffed and continued. "Within the first week, one of *those*—" she pointed at the origami frog, "had shown up. I came home from work and it was just sitting on the kitchen counter."

"A frog?" Gareth asked mildly.

"Not a *frog!*" she said disdainfully. "It was a butterfly. Made out of a receipt for building supplies. The next day there was some kind of bird in the bathroom. And then the next day—I made Javier search the house with a baseball bat, but there was no one here. Then we installed security cameras. All they showed was the damn things just suddenly appearing! So if there's no one hiding in the house, where are they coming from?! What kind of ghost spends all its time stealing paper and making origami animals?"

"That's what we're here to find out," I said, "Just stay in the living room for a bit. We're going to take a look around, see if we can sense anything unusual. What would you say is the exact centre of the house? We'll start from there."

"Probably the dining room," she waved at us dismissively. "You know, there are laws against things like this. If the real estate agent knew the place was haunted, she was *legally obligated* to tell us. If there really is a ghost here, I'm going to sue her."

Gareth and I looked at each other; he rolled his eyes subtly. "Dining room's as good a place to start as any," he said, picking up his bag.

We left her there on the sofa, hand over her eyes, and made our way through the kitchen to the dining room.

"Anything yet?" I asked Gareth.

He sniffed the air. "If I can get away from the stench of the Chanel she's wearing, I might be able to tell you." We walked out of the kitchen and stood in the door of the dining room. He closed his eyes and focused. "Still Chanel, but under it—Ivory soap…miso? And very faintly, fish."

"Interesting combination," I said, moving into the room. We stood in silence for a moment; the only sounds were far-off traffic and birds singing in the distance. Suddenly, I heard something closer, the rustling of paper. Gareth heard it too—he pointed at the dining room table. The rustling was coming from under it. I breathed in quietly, nervously, then got down on my hands and knees.

There was a tiny figure sitting under the table, hidden by the legs of the dining chairs. She was in shadow, but I crawled under the table closer to her, my heart beating hard. She was completely focused on the paper in her hands, fingers flying, as she folded and folded it into a shape. I sat back with my legs crossed and watched. Her head was down, long black hair obscuring her face. Then she made a final fold, held the paper to her lips and blew into it. She raised her head and held out the shape to me.

"It's a balloon," she whispered. Her eyes were deep brown and almond-shaped. She looked about seven years old, but her face was pale and there was blood around her mouth and nose. She was wearing a thin cotton dress with a rounded collar and a pink cardigan with tiny white, scalloped buttons. I took the origami balloon from her gently.

"What's your name?" I asked.

She smiled shyly. "Jenny," she whispered, "but Baba calls me Etsuko." She turned around as if to reach behind her, and a piece of paper magically appeared in her hands. It looked like a telephone bill. "I can make you something. Do you like stars?"

I nodded, and her fingers began flying again, folding the piece of paper into a complex shape. "Jenny," I asked, "what are you doing here?"

"I live here," she said matter-of-factly, as if it was the most normal thing in the world.

"How long have you been here?" I asked, watching her intensely. She stopped working the paper in her hands and stared at me.

"I don't know. I was asleep for a long time, and then I woke up. The lady doesn't like me. I keep giving her presents, but they just make her more angry. Baba loved my presents...before she went away."

"Where did Baba go?" I asked. Gareth was behind me, fidgeting, anxious. He hated that he couldn't see them — he could only sense the shimmer and smell the things they had left behind. "What about your mother and father?"

"The bad men came for us. They said we were traitors. They made Daddy work, and we were cold and I wanted to come home so badly. Then Baba got sick and she went away. After, I cried and cried. Everything was *so* cold and I started to cough. I went to bed and fell asleep. Then, I was here. The crashing woke me up."

I relayed to Gareth what the little girl had told me. He mulled it over for a second, then said, "The construction. It must have made her manifest. She came back to the last place she remembered being warm and safe."

Gareth's explanation made sense. I turned to Jenny.

"Jenny, the lady isn't mad at you, she's just scared. She can't see you, you know? You need to go and be with Baba."

The little girl's eyes filled with tears and she shook her head vigorously. "Baba is gone. I tried but I can't find her or Momma and Papa. Please don't make me go. I promise I'll be good and not scare the lady anymore."

I sighed and backed out from under the table. Gareth looked at me questioningly and gestured down towards the duffel bag that contained the box. "I don't know," I said. "She's frightened and she doesn't want to leave. She said she tried but she can't find her family."

"Can't find whose family?" Susan asked from the doorway. She stared down at me sitting cross-legged on her dining room carpet. "What are you doing?" She'd calmed down considerably, and now her face looked tired, drawn. "Have you figured out what's going on?"

"It's a little girl, Asian, about seven years old. Her name is Jenny." I said, holding up the origami balloon. "She's been making these for you as presents."

Her jaw dropped. "My—my house is haunted by a seven-year-old girl?! How the hell did she get here? Why?!"

"Etsuko is a Japanese name," Gareth said quietly. "Based on the age of the original house, she was probably sent to an internment camp with her family after Japan entered World War II. A lot of them, especially the children and the elderly, died from disease, a lot of them from tuberculosis. Maybe her parents were deported and that's why she can't find them."

I was surprised—it was the most I'd heard Gareth speak in front of a client in all the time I'd known him. What he said made sense though and I nodded in agreement. "She must have come here when the construction started. Chances are, her family home was the one you tore down to build this place. Spirits are often tethered back to where they feel safe. She's been trying to communicate with you in the only way she knows how."

Susan's eyes grew wide. "Communicate with me? That's what the paper animals are all about?" She put her hand against the doorframe as if to steady herself. "What—what do we do now?"

Gareth leaned over and picked up the duffel bag, and I stood up, stretching my back and shoulders, stiff from being hunched under the table. "Now," I said, "we try to help her on her way. It might be tricky—she's scared and she doesn't want to go. Gareth, I think you might have to use—"

"No!" Susan interjected. "Jenny doesn't have to go." She looked at us each in turn. "This was a mistake. Thanks very much, but I don't need your help."

"She can't stay here," Gareth said softly. "It isn't right." Gareth had a very black and white view of what we did. Me, I was a little more "live and let live" or, I suppose, "die and let die". I'd seen the joy on the faces of those who'd gone into the box, but I also knew that there were reasons why some chose to stay here with us. It wasn't for me to judge, and I certainly knew the pain of wanting to spend a few more minutes with someone before they were gone forever.

"What do you mean, 'she can't stay here'?" Susan demanded, the old attitude back full force. "It's *my* house and it's *my* decision. Again, thank you for your services—I'm happy to pay whatever you charge, but..." There was a pause, and then, suddenly, she started to sob. She put her hand up over her eyes and her chest heaved, then she turned and disappeared into the kitchen. We waited for a moment in silence, unsure what was happening. Jenny peeked out from under the table.

"Why is the lady so sad?" The origami star that she had just made was sitting on the carpet in front of her.

"I don't know," I said. "Maybe she needs a present to make her feel better." I turned to Susan, who had come back into the room still sniffling. "Put out your hand," I directed her.

She wiped her eyes with a tissue and stood there for a moment unmoving, uncertain. Then tentatively, she opened her other hand and reached out to the air. Suddenly, the origami star appeared, gently hovering just above her outstretched palm. She gasped, and curled her fingers around it, then held it up to look at it, tears still running down her face. "You know," she said, "Javier and I tried for so long to have children. Maybe she—Jenny—is here for a reason. Maybe I need her as much as she needs me."

Gareth shrugged in resignation and picked up his duffel bag. "Call us if you ever change your mind," he said. But Susan wasn't listening—she was down on her hands and knees peering under the dining room table.

"I'm going to get you some proper origami paper," she said. Jenny smiled widely, her almond-shaped eyes full of excitement and hope.

"She said her Baba called her 'Etsuko'. I think she might like that," I offered.

Jenny nodded happily and Susan smiled. "Etsuko, it is," she said, backing out from under the table.

The little girl crawled out after her and stood up straight. She was tiny for seven years, delicate and heartbreaking in her pink cardigan with the tiny white buttons.

"I just have one last thing I need to do," I said to Susan. "Can you give us a minute?"

Susan left the room, glancing back over her shoulder as if she could see the small figure standing there. She waved and said, "I'll just be in the kitchen if you need me," and I wasn't sure if she was talking to me or Etsuko. But I had a question I needed to ask.

"Etsuko, have you ever seen another little girl, maybe a bit younger than you? She's wearing a T-shirt with a unicorn on it." She looked uncertain so I added, "A unicorn is like a horse but it has a horn on the top of its head. It's very sparkly."

She thought for a moment and then her dark eyes widened. "The man said I'm not supposed to tell anyone.

He wanted me to go too but I said no, I needed to wait for Baba."

"What man?!" I exclaimed. "Who was she with?"

Suddenly, her smile fell and her eyes became fixed on some point far away. "Oni. It was Oni. He had on his devil mask. I was afraid but then he took it off and he looked like one of the bad men, and that made me angry. He wanted me to come with him too but I said I needed to stay here. The other girl was afraid and crying. She wanted her sister but I couldn't help her. I gave her a present, a horse like the one on her shirt. Oni wanted to burn it, but she said "No!" He said, 'Our money, you can't take this with you where we're going,' but she did anyway."

"Our *money*?" I asked.

"Not our money. 'Armony."

I felt as though someone had punched me in the throat—I couldn't breathe, and a scream filled my head. 'Armony? Harmony. Whoever it was, he had Harmony.

6

GARETH WINTER

As told to Verity Darkwood one evening while very drunk.

Gareth Winter was born, ironically, in the spring, during a flood. As the water of the Otter Creek rose up around the midwife's feet, he came into the world with one cry, then was silent. Almost immediately, the water began to recede, causing his father, who was a lay minister, to insist that he be named Gregory, like the saint, but his mother refused. She was a woman of science herself, and had her heart settled on Gareth, after her brother who had died as a child.

When he was eight years old, Gareth began to have nightmares so realistic that he would wake up shaking with fear. He never cried out; it wasn't in his nature to say much, and he didn't want to wake his little sister Julia, who at four years old, was asleep in a cot in the corner because the new baby needed her room. But one morning at breakfast, his mother, who had heard him pacing in the hallway when the moon was still up, asked him what was wrong.

"Nothing," he said.

"Are you having bad dreams?"

He nodded. His mother put down the baby she was nursing, his second sister Dawn Marie, walked over to him and took his face between her hands. "Dreams are just the brain's way of working out problems. You can control your dreams if you want to. The next time something tries to scare you in a dream, laugh at it and tell it to go away."

Gareth's father looked up from the newspaper and put down his coffee mug. "Nonsense," he scoffed. "Dreams are the Lord's way of warning you. Listen to your dreams and take heed." Then he picked his coffee mug back up and continued reading. Gareth's mother's mouth tightened. She rolled her eyes, handed back the crayon Julia had just dropped on the floor, and sighed as she cradled the baby in her arms. Nothing more was said on the subject.

Two nights later, the dream came again. He was standing on the bank of the Otter Creek out behind his house. The water was dark and swirling, and as he stared into its depths, another face swam into the eddies next to his own. It was the face of a man, a regular-looking man in every way except for his eyes. His eyes were yellow. Gareth turned his head and the man was standing next to him as real as anything Gareth had ever seen. The man was wearing regular-looking clothes—a tan jacket and khaki pants—like anyone would wear. The only thing that distinguished him as a creature from a nightmare was the sulphur that flashed in his eyes. Gareth, leaning towards the science side of things, did as his mother suggested. "Go away," he demanded, his eight-year-old voice reedy and high-pitched.

The regular-looking nightmare man laughed, his exposed teeth looking sharper than normal. "I don't think so," he said. It was a regular-sounding voice too, but underneath it was a more guttural sound, a low liquid growl.

Gareth decided to take his father's tack. "Why are you here?"

The man laughed again. "Don't get too close to the edge," he warned. "The water is deep and cold. And you're not the one I want." He held out his hand and in it was a small, striped rubber ball. He tossed it into the air and caught it, once, twice, then he paused. He gave Gareth a cunning smile as he turned and threw the ball into the creek.

"GO AWAY!" Gareth yelled again. This force of his voice seemed to make the nightmare man take a step back. He cocked his head to one side and looked puzzled. Then he smirked and said, "We'll see, little hunter." He began to howl with laughter and the sound grew louder and filled Gareth's ears until they ached. He clapped his hands over them and fell to the ground, eyes squeezed shut. The laughter stopped suddenly; Gareth opened his eyes and looked around but the man had disappeared. Gareth was immobilized. The dark water of the creek began to rise and just as it reached the tips of his shoes, he woke up.

The dream convinced him that his mother was wrong. He couldn't control what happened while he was asleep any more than, at eight years old, he could control what happened when he was awake. He wouldn't realize that he should have listened to his father until a few weeks later when his mother was out back hanging clothes on the line and lost sight of Julia. "I don't understand!" his mother cried, bewildered and terrified. "She would never have wandered off on her own!"

When they pulled his baby sister's petite body out of the Otter Creek two days later after a frantic search, his mother screamed and fainted. His father sank to his knees, calling out to the heavens, "Why Lord, why?!" and began to weep, wrenching sobs shaking his body. Gareth just stood there, his child's eyes wide with shock. Julia's body was surrounded by adults—police officers who had combed the surrounding woodlands, neighbours who had come to offer what comfort they could and to care for Gareth and the baby. Finally, there were the divers who had pulled the tiny figure out of the water, carrying her carefully up the steep bank, and laying her gently on the ground. As the crowd parted slightly, he glimpsed her, dress water-logged and shoes still dripping. Then one of the neighbours turned away and Gareth could see that Julia was holding something in her hand. He took a step forward and gasped as he realized that her fingers were curled tight around a striped rubber ball.

That night, Gareth put himself to bed. His mother was exhausted from weeping and she sat in the living room in the dark, holding the baby and refusing any food. His father wandered through the house, eyes swollen, his faith shaken. Gareth, unobtrusive even at 8 years old, had made himself a peanut butter and jam sandwich, then brushed his teeth and crawled under the covers, trying not to look at the little cot in the corner of his room. He lay there for a long time, flat on his back, covers pulled up to his chin, afraid to sleep. He knew the man was waiting. But he wasn't afraid of the man anymore; he was afraid of what he might do to the man, and he wondered if he could carry a knife into his dream and stab the man through the heart. Finally, his eyelids fluttered and closed, and he fell into a deep sleep.

He awoke suddenly, eyes wide. He breathed in deeply and as he did, he realized that the air was filled with the scent of baby powder mixed with a more dank smell—creek water. He turned slowly to the cot, terrified that he would see Julia, her skin blue, her clothes dripping, but instead there was a strange shimmer, an area where all the light had been sucked away except for flecks that sparkled against the darkness. As he stared, a shape emerged from the shimmer—and then he heard something bouncing on the wooden floor towards his bed. He leaned down and scooped up the object—it was the striped rubber ball. He inhaled sharply, making a quiet, high-pitched whimper.

"Julia?" he whispered, and the shimmer pulsated. He was trembling, caught somewhere between terror and excitement. He didn't know much about death. The year before, their good-natured retriever Sergeant had become very ill and stopped eating. His father had taken Sergeant to the vet, but when he came home, it was without the dog. When Gareth asked what had happened, his father replied, "The good Lord has taken him into his care" and his mother, eyes too teary to roll, sighed and said, "Sergeant was old and very tired. He's gone to sleep now, and he doesn't have to worry about being sick anymore."

When Gareth asked, "Will he wake up and come back?", both his parents, despite their contrasting explanations, were quick to say, "Oh no — he's gone to a better place."

Gareth had struggled with the idea that Sergeant could possibly be in a better place than lying under the kitchen table hoping for scraps, or curled up in front of the fire, but after a few days, it seemed his parents were correct because Sergeant never came back. But if his parents *were* right, why was Julia shimmering from the cot in the corner of his bedroom?

The next three nights were difficult for Gareth. He would close his eyes, wake up from a dreamless sleep, and there would be the shimmer, sparkling in the corner. On the fourth day after Julia was pulled from the creek, the funeral was held. His mother explained that he wouldn't see Julia, that she was in a casket, a special box made just for her, but that he could still say goodbye to her. He stood in the receiving line wide-eyed, his father stoic next to him, his mother sobbing.

"It was my fault," she told the neighbours, who murmured tearful words of comfort.

"I should never have taken my eyes off her!" she cried to Gareth's aunt, who hugged her tight.

"I'll never forgive myself," she whispered to the picture of Julia atop the tragically small casket. In the picture, Julia was all dimples, a yellow bow in her hair, her bright blue eyes twinkling. "Never," she whispered again, stroking the glass as if it was Julia's little cheek.

That night, Gareth was certain that he would no longer be visited by the shimmer. They had said goodbye to Julia in her box and she was in a better place now, so everyone said. He fell into a deep sleep once again, but once again, he woke up like a shot a few hours later. He kept his eyes shut tight but even through his closed lids, he could see the shimmer illuminating his room. He could also hear something, as if from far away—it was the sound of his mother crying. Ignoring the shimmer for a moment, he pulled back the covers, got out of bed, and padded down the hallway to the living room where his mother sat in the dark, hunched over and shaking with grief. He silently slid up onto the couch beside her and she put her arm around him.

"It's all my fault," she said again. "How can I ever forgive myself?" Gareth desperately wanted to tell her it wasn't true, that it was the man's fault, the regular-looking man from his dream, but even at the age of 8, he knew she wouldn't understand. He took her hand and sat with her for a while until finally, she wiped her eyes with a soggy tissue and said, "Let's get you back to bed."

He had a moment of panic as they walked down the hall, but when they got to his room, his mother didn't seem to notice the shimmer in the corner. At the sight of her, it pulsated more strongly. His mother tucked him into bed, kissed him and left. He turned to the shimmer and addressed it. "Momma's sad," he said. "She says it's her fault that you fell in the creek, but I know it's not. Is that why you're here?" The shimmer glowed more strongly. "We have to figure out a way to let her know that she shouldn't blame herself."

The next day, he had a brainwave. He got the craft box out of the cupboard, the box full of paper, crayons, and other art supplies that his mother kept for rainy days, and he tucked it under his bed for later. When he woke up in the night, the shimmer was there waiting. He pulled the craft box from under the bed and took out a piece of paper and some crayons.

"Here," he said, offering them to the air in front of him. "You can make Momma a picture so she knows you're not mad at her." Nothing happened, so he moved closer to the shimmer. Still nothing, Finally, impatient, he thrust the paper and crayons right into it. They disappeared. He went back and sat down on his bed to wait. His eyelids grew heavy, and his head started to nod. Suddenly, there was a clatter of crayons dropping to the ground, and the piece of paper reappeared, wafting gently on invisible currents. He jumped up and snatched it out of the air. In the dim light, he could make out the picture that wasn't there before, a little stick figure girl holding hands with a stick figure woman. They were enclosed by a lopsided red heart and the words "I luv you mommy" were scrawled in childish letters across the bottom.

"Momma will be so happy," he said, and the shimmer glowed and pulsed. "Maybe," he ventured. "...maybe you can live in the craft box so if Momma gets sad again, you could make her another picture." He opened the lid of the box and the shimmer moved forward slowly. He held the box up towards it, closer, and the shimmer seemed to constrict and lengthen. Finally, it flowed into the craft box and the room, deprived of its glow, was plunged into darkness. Gareth sighed, shut the lid, and then shoved the box back under the bed as far as it would go, hidden from everyone but him.

The next morning, the first thing Gareth did was look at the picture to make sure he hadn't been dreaming. But there they were — the stick figure little girl and her mother, the heart, the words so lovingly etched onto the paper. He took it with him to breakfast. His mother was sitting in her place, nursing Dawn Marie, and his father was reading the paper and drinking coffee, like they did every morning. The only thing missing was Julia. Gareth softly placed the picture at Julia's place and tapped his mother's arm.

"What is it, Gareth?" she asked wearily.

"Julia made this for you. She doesn't want you to be sad anymore."

His mother stared at the picture for a moment and then tears rolled down her face. "Gareth Winter," she said, her voice breaking, "you are the sweetest boy I know. Thank you for making this for me—it really means a lot."

Gareth opened his mouth to protest then hesitated. Even at 8 years old, he knew it was better not to say anything. If his mother couldn't believe that Julia drew her a picture, she'd certainly *never* understand that Julia was living in the craft box under his bed.

Of course, that night, when he opened the box to tell Julia that Momma had loved the picture, he was heartbroken to discover she was gone. He didn't realize until he was much older that, had he not put her in the craft box, she might still have been with him. Momma's guilt was nothing compared to Gareth's. She'd lost Julia once; Gareth Winter had lost her twice.

7

POLTERGEIST PAT

Dear DarkWinter Direct:
    I recently saw your ad in The Echo: A Journal for Lovers of the Macabre, and decided to contact you about a problem I've been having. I wasn't sure at first, but I got in touch with the editor, Horace Greeley III, and he vouched for you. So here's my story.
    I've always been open to the idea of a spirit world, and the possibility that there are forces in this universe that we can't fully understand. For example, five years ago, we rented one side of a 100-year-old "twin home", which is like a semi-detached house. The old basement didn't look dangerous but it felt that way, like someone was watching you, and I avoided going down there like the plague. After a couple of months, we moved into the other side of the house. Same layout, same type and age of basement, only I had no problem going down there at all. No bad vibes whatsoever. Then we bought our current house in Washington (Ontario, not DC). It's a huge old Georgian-style place, built in 1863, and pretty run down, having been empty for almost two years after the 70-year-old owner passed away. I didn't sense anything unusual when we first toured it, but that soon changed.

We began renovating immediately, starting with the upstairs bathroom. It had been built into a partitioned-off back bedroom, which became our baby's room. The bathroom walls were clad in pressure-treated boards, and it had a wall sink, a clawfoot tub, and an old swag lamp for lighting. Totally creepy, dark, and dingy. After redoing the walls with board and batten, painting the whole thing white and updating the fixtures (including a new medicine cabinet), it was much more livable. For us **and** for the obnoxious poltergeist who occupied it. Yes, I said "poltergeist". And it was one with a very juvenile sense of humour. It wasn't long before things started flying out of the new medicine cabinet. And I don't mean "falling out", I mean a kind of forceful lobbing. If I had a dollar for every time I got hit with a hairbrush, or my toothbrush flew into the toilet, I'd be a rich woman. There was a built-in cupboard in the corner with upper and lower doors – sometimes if you bent down to get something out of the lower cabinet, when you went to stand up, the upper doors would be suddenly open and you'd crack your head on them. Of course, my husband was totally skeptical, having his own POLTERGEIST-FREE bathroom on the main floor.

"Maybe the gravity is just weird in there," he'd say. "Or maybe the walls are on an angle or something." But there were two other notable incidents that made me believe that it was more ghost than gravity:

1) One night, I woke up around 1 in the morning. My husband, Chris, hadn't come to bed yet, and as I was lying there, I could hear sounds coming from the baby monitor. Our daughter, who was about two at the time, was talking to someone. I yelled "Chris! What are you doing? It's one o'clock in the morning – why are you in Kate's room?" No answer. I called a couple of more times. I could still hear Kate talking and a man's voice replying, so finally, I got ticked off and stomped into her room. There was no one there. Kate just kind of looked at me, then closed her eyes and went back to sleep. I totally lost it and went running around the house (it was a really big old house) looking for Chris. I finally found him in the family room downstairs. "There was

someone in Kate's room!" I said, and told him what happened. He grabbed a baseball bat, and we searched the house, but we didn't find anyone. After we calmed down, Chris got all rational.

"There are two possible explanations," he said. "Either you were still asleep and dreamed it, or there's another baby monitor in town and ours was picking up someone else's frequency." Neither of those reasons made any sense though – first, I was wide awake, and second, Kate was the first baby in the community in about 12 years, so nobody else had a baby monitor for miles. I know a lot of people are creeped out by baby monitors – and there's good justification for that as far as I'm concerned.

2) We have a guest bedroom next to the baby's room, and every once in a while, it smells like cigarette smoke, even though we've repainted it, and no one in our family smokes. One night, I had a really bad cough and, not wanting to disturb Chris, I decided to sleep in there. I woke up coughing around 3 in the morning, and as I was lying there, I heard the distinct sound of the baby gate at the top of the stairs being opened. It was a super-secure gate, and to open it, you had to push down hard on the handle, slide it back, then swing it open. And that was the exact sound I'd just heard – click, slide, swing. I lay there, paralysed with fear, thinking that someone had broken into the house, and waited to hear footsteps before I started screaming (the floorboards were very old and creaky, so if anyone was upstairs, I'd know it in a second). I waited – nothing else happened, so after a while, I just kind of fell back to sleep. But in the morning, I went out into the hall, and the baby gate was wide open.

Now, you might think this was all in my imagination, but I know it wasn't. A couple of weeks after the incident with the baby gate, we were having a garage sale, and a very elderly man drove up. He struck up a conversation with us, said that he'd grown up in our area and that he knew our house quite well.

"Funny story," he said. "My Uncle Pat lived right here in this house for most of his life – he was the last owner before the people you bought from. He was over eighty when he died. He got 'funny' towards the end – a real practical joker. His favourite trick was to put on a clown mask, then sneak up to the church when the Ladies' Choir was practicing. He'd peek in the windows and just about scare them to death, then run away laughing! Of course, it was the cancer that got him in the end — he was a chain smoker, you know."

After hearing his story about Uncle Pat, and seeing the ad for Darkwinter Direct, I decided to contact you. Is this the type of thing you can help me with? I'm getting really worried about the baby's safety.

Sincerely,
Tanis Gibson

"Cute," I said, glancing around at the white-washed board and batten walls, the stencilled clawfoot tub, and the large, new medicine cabinet. Gareth and I were standing in the very small bathroom of a house in Washington, a place not so much a village as a crossroads, in rural Ontario.

"Anything?" Gareth asked.

"Not yet." I hesitated. Even though I knew that Gareth always took me at my word, after years of my mother's doubts, I was still reluctant to voice my feelings.

Gareth turned to me, interest piqued. "What?"

I tried to articulate how it felt, that clenching in my chest, that sense of my mind being polluted like black ink bleeding into clear water, signalling something not quite right. Usually, if I stared at one of the bad houses long enough, the water became completely tainted, but in this place, the negative energy ebbed and flowed. When we pulled up and I got my first impression, everything seemed fine. Then I checked the time on my phone, and when I looked back up at the house, I was overcome with an ominous disorientation. I blinked hard, and when I opened my eyes again, everything was back to normal.

"It's almost like the house is in flux. One minute it's fine, the next minute it's gone dark."

Suddenly I felt a cold rush, and a rough voice said, "You're telling me!"

Gareth whipped his head around—he must have caught the shimmer that had apparated without warning. I followed Gareth's gaze and was stunned to see a figure lounging in the clawfoot bathtub, one elbow resting on the ledge, long legs dangling over the end. The figure wore a latex clown mask, garishly painted, with an evil toothy grin and a mop of red synthetic hair on the top. I involuntarily jumped and the figure laughed, a low, dark cackle. I took a step back, and then the cackle turned into a merry chuckle as the figure removed the mask. Beneath it was the rather pleasant-looking face of an elderly man, green eyes twinkling and face creased from laughter.

"Didn't mean to scare you," he said, waving the mask airily at us. "Didn't know you could see me." He pulled himself up, got out of the tub and perched on the ledge.

"Uncle Pat, I presume," I addressed him.

"Maybe," he answered coyly, shrugging his shoulders. He folded up the clown mask and shoved it into the back pocket of his jeans. "Who wants to know?"

"I'm Verity. This is Gareth." Gareth nodded his sharp chin in greeting towards the bathtub, unable to see or hear Uncle Pat, but aware of his presence. "The people who are living in this house asked us to come."

"Did they now?" His brow furrowed. "It's about bloody time. Shit or get off the pot, I say."

I was confused. "I don't understand," I said. "Why are you giving Tanis so much trouble? The toothbrushes, hairbrushes, all the things you've been throwing around in here—why are you attacking her?"

"Attacking her?!" he sputtered, outraged, and leapt up. "Attack—I've been trying to *warn* her!"

I took a step back as he moved towards me, and Gareth put a hand on my shoulder protectively. "What's going on?" he asked. "The bag is just outside the door—do I need to get it?"

With that, Uncle Pat stopped advancing. His eyes were still blazing, but it was more the anger of being misunderstood than aggression. "No," I answered without looking at Gareth. "He says he's not attacking Tanis, he's trying to warn her. Warn her about what?"

"About the baby!" he shouted. "Do you think it's easy, trying to keep her safe from him? It's not like I have a lot of options when it comes to getting someone's attention, you know!" He made a sweeping gesture with his index finger and the medicine cabinet door flew open. A hairbrush came soaring through the air, narrowly missing Gareth's ear.

"Hey!" Gareth yelled. He took two long strides into the hallway and picked up his bag. "I think it's time, Verity," he announced, wielding it in front of him like a shield as Uncle Pat gestured again and a bottle of contact lens cleaner shot towards him. "What the hell!"

"Ok, let's just calm down," I called out over the two men. Gareth stopped outside the bathroom door, bag protecting his face and torso, breathing hard. Uncle Pat pursed his lips together in consternation but lowered his arm. "You said you were trying to protect Kate from 'him'. Who is 'him'?"

"John Berith." He spat it out as if the name left a bad taste in his mouth. "That one's always hanging around here, waiting for the mother to take her eyes off the little girl for a second. I can't go much further than these few rooms up here, but I do my best to make sure they're paying attention."

I looked around and shivered. Another presence here would certainly account for the ambiguity I was feeling. The house was caught in a veritable tug of war between Uncle Pat's positive energy and another, darker force. "What does he want with her?"

"I have no goddamned idea!" Uncle Pat exclaimed. "But he's always trying to give her things, toys you know, to get her to follow him out to the pond." He pointed to the small window in the far wall of the bathroom. In the distance, I could see water glinting in the sunlight through the trees. "It's deep," he continued, "and I should know. I had it dug out years ago and sold the clay for bricks. Gotta be twelve feet down in the middle. Not a place for a little girl to wander off to. The bastard came sniffing around the other day, trying to talk to her through that walkie talkie thing, and I'd had my fill of it. I don't know how, being on different 'planes' or whatever you call it, but I was able to appear to him—I told him to piss off or he'd have to deal with me! Haven't seen him since."

A throat cleared behind me. "Sorry," I said, forgetting Gareth had no idea what was happening. "Have you ever heard the name 'John Berith'? Apparently, he's been coming around and trying to lure Kate down to the pond. Uncle Pat's been acting all poltergeisty to get Tanis's attention and protect the little girl. He's not trying to hurt anyone."

Gareth looked towards the ceiling, a signal that he was thinking and trying to recall the name. "John Berith?" he said finally. "The only Berith I know is a demon from the Old Testament."

"Well, that's all fine and good," scoffed Uncle Pat, "but he doesn't *look* like a demon. In fact, he's the most regular-looking fella I've ever seen. Except for those eyes. Sickly and yellow, they are."

His words made my blood run cold. Gareth and I had encountered the ordinary man with the sulphur eyes individually and together on more than one occasion. We looked at each other with trepidation. Pat saw the look and laughed breezily. "Don't get your knickers in a knot. He's hit the road. And if he ever comes back, I'll be here." He yelled out to Gareth, "So you can put your pretty box away—I'm not going anywhere."

I was quiet for a minute, concentrating and reaching out with my mind. Everything seemed clean, but just on the edges, there was a darkness lurking, like one of Mr. Wiggle's minions waiting around the corner, and I suddenly had some doubts that John Berith, whoever or whatever he was, had been completely banished. "There's still something here," I murmured to Gareth. He understood what I was going to say next. He placed the bag back down onto the floor and nodded his assent.

"All right," I turned to Uncle Pat. "It'd be better if you stayed for a while. But you have to promise to stop throwing things unless he comes back. Spend your time figuring out a better way to communicate, how about that?"

"Hah!" he snorted and rolled his eyes. "Maybe I can figure out how to use that walkie-talkie thing. Wouldn't *that* be a good trick?"

"Absolutely not," I said. "People think baby monitors are spooky enough already. Just…behave yourself. I'm telling Tanis that we think you're gone, but she's to call us the second anything else strange happens. Got it?"

Uncle Pat pulled the clown mask out of his back pocket and put it on. "Got it," he leered at us, then snapped his fingers and vanished.

"Let's go," I said to Gareth. "Although I don't think we should take payment for this. I mean, we didn't actually get rid of him."

Gareth stared at me. "I hope you're joking. I almost lost an eye. We definitely deserve the money. Now hurry up and collect it—I have some research to do. And when you send the details to Horace…don't tell him about John Berith."

8

HORACE GREELEY III

Gareth and I were introduced to Horace Greeley III not long after we'd first met at the bar in Kincardine. When we'd both recovered from our hangovers, we talked for a long time about what we should do moving forward. It was obvious we made a good team—in fact, Gareth, in an unusually emotional way (at least when he was sober) had announced that he had been waiting for someone like me for a very long time. It wasn't until much further along in our relationship that I discovered he'd been waiting for me specifically in Milly's that night—how he knew that I'd be there is a story for another day. Regardless, we clicked, and after months on the road and being literally close to the end of my rope, I needed him as much as he needed me.

The plan was simple at first. We would advertise on social media 'buy and sell' sites and hope to drum up a little business as...well, we didn't know exactly as *what*; I mean, what do you call yourselves in our situation without sounding like something out of a bad reality show? Gareth had an old laptop, and I set up a simple website we named DarkWinter, making everything as vague as possible to see what kind of response we would get. The response was underwhelming. The initial excitement we'd both felt when the website went live was soon replaced by discouragement, as we went from job to job and found nothing except figments of overactive imaginations or religious paranoia. The number of people who *think* they've seen a ghost far outweighs the number of people who actually have.

The day we encountered Horace, we were in Etobicoke, a suburb of Toronto, standing in front of the door to a small walk-in closet, while two middle-aged men huddled together in anticipation on the other side of the room.

"I'm sure there's something in there," the taller one whispered. "The ceiling light has a motion sensor, and I never get up in the middle of the night, do I, Rico?"

"Never!" Rico, the shorter, more rotund member of the duo responded emphatically. "And sweetie, that door is *always* kept closed, except when we're in there, of course. Donny is claustrophobic."

"*Closet*-trophobic!" Donny exclaimed, and they both started laughing riotously. Gareth shot them a sharp look and they immediately stopped. "Sorry," Donny whispered. "We just don't know how the light is coming on by itself in the middle of the night. It must be a—a spirit!"

"It must be," Rico nodded his head vigorously. "There's no other explanation. It's happened three times in the past two weeks. And now we're both afraid to open the door, but we need to get in there!"

"All right," I said. "Here we go." I reached for the door handle and both men gasped and took two quick steps back in tandem. I rolled my eyes inwardly and flung the door open. The light flashed on, and Gareth and I both did a double-take at the contents of the closet; it was overflowing with gowns, wigs, and high heels. I'd never seen so many sequins in my life. The effect was dazzling, and I practically had to shield my eyes. Gareth started to say something and then stopped. We both looked at Rico and Donny.

"Oh!" Donny said. "I suppose we should have mentioned that we're both drag queens."

"At the Palladium in Toronto," Rico added proudly. "I'm Mabel Syrup! I don't know if you're familiar with my work."

"No, not really, sorry." I'd never seen a drag show in person, but I'd seen drag queens on TV. "What's *your* stage name?" I asked Donny.

He looked at the floor shyly. "I'm Connie Canuck." He hesitated, then looked up and batted his eyes coquettishly. "Maybe you've heard of *me*?"

Gareth's eyes widened. "You're Connie Canuck? Didn't you used to have that talk show on CBC when you were younger?"

"Younger! It was only eight years ago—no need to get shady!" Connie/Donny flared his nostrils indignantly.

Gareth muttered an apology. I was already in the closet, having no idea who Connie Canuck was, trying to concentrate. I couldn't sense anything at all, not even a flicker. I crouched down, trying to see under the skirts of the billowing ballgowns that were compressed tightly together, when I noticed something behind a rhinestone stiletto. There were tiny droppings in the corner. I straightened up. "I think I know what's been triggering your motion sensor," I said.

Rico gasped and turned to Donny. "Someone died in this house! I knew it! We're putting this place on the market, girl!"

"Wait—hang on!" I interrupted as the two men began to argue. "It's not a spirit. You've got mice."

"*Mice*?!" shrieked Donny, horrified. "That's even worse than a ghost!! You were right, Rico—call the real estate agent."

"Better to call an exterminator," Gareth said flatly. "Or buy a mousetrap. We won't charge you the full amount. Fifty dollars is fine."

Later, back in the trailer, we took stock. "So far this month, we've made $127.00. That barely covers our gas," I sighed. "It's okay though—we can go somewhere touristy for a couple of days and I can busk."

Gareth shook his head. "Something better will come along, I just know it. Check the inbox."

"What's the point?" I asked. "It'll just be another séance request or…or rodent invasion." I opened the laptop and clicked on the email icon anyway. "Huh. This might be promising."

The email was composed in a fancy font, as if the sender was writing it by hand. *Dear Ms. Darkwood and Mr. Winter*, it read. *I hope this finds you well. While I don't mean to intrude and while it's certainly not my place to interfere, it occurs to me that your talents are, perhaps, not reaching the right audience. I have a proposition for you. If you find yourself at loose ends and in the Collingwood area, please feel free to drop by for a sherry. Best of Regards, Horace Greeley III.* There was a street address listed below the message.

"Interesting," Gareth said.

"Collingwood, hmm? It wouldn't hurt to check this out. At worst, it's a tourist town, and I could earn some cash with the old guitar. How long do you think it'll take to get there from Etobicoke?"

Gareth checked Google Maps. "We can be there in under 2 hours. There are a couple of good campsites outside the town."

"OK. I'll message this Horace guy back and see if he's free tomorrow. That way we can get there by dinnertime, set up a site, and check out the town first."

Horace responded to my email almost right away, as if he somehow knew that he'd piqued our interest and was just waiting for a response. Gareth and I packed up the trailer, then we got in the truck. The strain on the engine as we pulled away was palpable—we were still hauling my old Tempo behind the fifth wheel. I couldn't sell the damned car, not even for scrap, since I didn't actually own it, and I couldn't just abandon it for fear that my parents would be notified and try to track me down. Regardless of the way we felt about each other, after what they'd gone through with Harmony, I felt bad enough about putting them through the disappearance of another daughter, and while I was almost 100% certain that they had no interest in my whereabouts, I didn't relish the thought of having them show up one day. And knowing my mother, if I explained to her what I'd been up to, she'd most likely try to have me committed. Can you imagine the conversation? "Oh yes, Mom, I've been traveling across the country with this middle-aged man—strictly platonic, Mom, don't worry—and we use the things in his magic bag to exorcise demons and help spirits caught in our plane to cross over. Is it scary? Well, a little at first but you get used to it." No, better to keep hauling the old rust bucket along with us—at least it came in handy when we needed more efficient, or inconspicuous, transport.

We got to Craigleith Provincial Park just outside of Blue Mountain around 6 pm. Because it was Tuesday, it was still early enough in the week that we were able to get one of the last campsites, so we set up quickly, then unhitched the Tempo and drove into Collingwood. Gareth had the idea that he wanted to check out Horace Greeley III first, so we headed for the heritage district. The address was on Pine Street, and as we cruised by the house number in the address that Horace had sent us, Gareth gave a low whistle.

"Wow," I agreed. The house was a stunning Victorian mansion, with turrets, a fancy slate roof, stained glass windows, and an upper balcony with French doors. The carefully manicured front lawn was surrounded by a black, wrought iron fence, and in the middle of the lawn was an impressive, custom-made wooden sign that simply said, "The Echo".

"His house is called 'The Echo'? Or is that a business?" I wondered out loud.

"Interesting," Gareth mused.

We parked down the street and watched the house for a while but there was no sign of any activity. Finally, after a couple with two small children walked by and gave the Tempo a suspicious look, we left. We didn't want to attract any more attention so we headed back towards the campsite, stopping at a roadside burger place. I ordered for both of us at the counter, laughing inwardly when the waitress asked, "Does your dad want onions with his burger?"

There were only about twenty-five years between me and Gareth, but I vastly preferred it when people thought he was my father rather than my boyfriend. Gareth was always appalled when he was asked if I was his daughter. "Do I really look *that* old?" he'd say to me later. It was his one small vanity, so I always reassured him that no, he didn't. In truth, he looked more world-weary than anything else, which made people assume he was older than he really was.

Horace Greeley III had invited us to 'luncheon' the next day, so we headed back to the Victorian mansion, parking right outside this time. We'd just reached the top step of the porch when the door was flung open by a man who bore a remarkable resemblance to the White Rabbit from *Alice in Wonderland*. His hair was lustrous and silver, and he was wearing a plaid waistcoat and a bright red topcoat. He had an ascot tied around his neck, and a gold chain from what I could only assume was a pocket watch swung from his waistcoat pocket.

"Hello, hello!" he called out effusively. He pulled the watch out of his pocket, confirming my assumption, and flipped open the lid. "Ms. Darkwood and Mr. Winter. You're right on time!" he announced, flashing the timepiece at us with a flourish. "Do come in!"

Gareth and I glanced at each other—he shrugged non-committally. Together, we walked past Horace into the recesses of the mansion. It was just as beautiful inside as it was on the outside, with carved wood trim, plush furniture, high ceilings, and crystal chandeliers. A circular staircase wound up towards a second story. There was so much to take in that I barely noticed as we made our formal introductions, then Horace ushered us into his "parlour", where luncheon waited.

In all my life, I'd never met anyone like Horace Greeley III. I can't even remember what we ate that day, except it was delicious, and I would have accepted his offering of seconds if Gareth hadn't interrupted and asked brusquely if Horace would be so kind as to explain why he invited us.

"Oh, of course!" Horace answered, not offended in the least. "I've been tracking you for a while—" He stopped when he saw my panicked look, and Gareth's scowl. "Now, by tracking, I simply mean following your...adventures, that's all. Nothing sinister here, I *assure* you!"

We both relaxed and he continued. "I have a lot of contacts due to the magazine—oh, I should probably explain about that first. I'm the very proud editor of *The Echo: A Journal for Lovers of the Macabre*." He waved his hand around airily. "This house is the headquarters, my little corner of the publishing world, where I gather tales of spirits, demons, and other supernatural splendors for my readers. I've seen your ads, and I've also heard that you haven't had much success so far—"

"What?" Gareth interjected.

"No, no, it's nothing to be ashamed of, my dear Gareth! It's exceedingly difficult for *anyone* to find success through those commonplace public sites, let alone true professionals like yourselves. The calibre of clientele is quite mundane, I know. That's why I've got a proposition for you."

There was a long pause. Gareth looked stormy; the expression on Horace's face was one of anticipation. I finally broke the silence. "Fair enough," I interjected. "I don't know how you've found out so much about us, but you're right. We haven't had a lot of luck so far with the cases we've been asked to investigate. So what did you have in mind?"

"Well, Verity," Horace's anticipation turned to outright glee. "Here's what I'm thinking. It's becoming increasingly more difficult for me to source out good material. There just aren't many people who do what you do, and I like my content to be as authentic as possible. At the same time, you need a better conduit between DarkWinter Direct and those who genuinely need your help, and that's where *The Echo* comes in. I'll offer you free advertising in my journal *and* assistance in vetting respondents. In exchange, you'll provide me with the details of your exploits, which I can wordsmith into something thrilling for my readers. What say you?"

Gareth and I looked at each other. I gave a slight nod. "Why not?" Gareth said. "Free advertising? Can't hurt."

Horace leapt out of his chair, clapping his hands together in delight. "Wonderful! I'll get the sherry, and we can toast our new partnership!" He left the room.

We waited a moment, then Gareth asked, "Thoughts?"

"I agree. It definitely can't hurt. Especially if he has 'connections'. If it doesn't work, we can always bail."

As it turned out though, Horace was a godsend. His eccentric outward appearance and behaviour hid an astute, business-like mind. By the end of that afternoon, we had a new website design, an intriguing ad in *The Echo*, and a tiered fee structure that, if everything worked the way Horace assured us, would provide enough funding to keep us on the road and well-fed.

"Five hundred dollars for the first hour?" I asked incredulously. "Who'll pay that?"

"Who wouldn't?" Horace replied. "For professionals such as yourselves? I know about Kincardine—don't ask me how, that's my little secret — and I'll be your reference until you've established a reputation, which I'm sure won't take long at all. Now, I have something special for you." He paused expectantly. "Oh, I can't wait to tell you — it's your first case! I was recently contacted by a man whose elderly mother passed away — and she won't leave him alone. Apparently, the nagging is even worse than it was when she was alive now that she can walk through walls. Not a moment of peace for poor Harold!"

Horace rubbed his hands together gleefully. I glanced at Gareth. He gave a slight shrug, as if to say, "Why not?"

Our partnership confirmed, Horace generously agreed to store the Tempo in the two-story barn-style garage behind his house. "No need to drag around the past," he laughed. "The future awaits!" I wasn't sorry to leave the old Ford in Horace's care. It wasn't just the weight of the car but the memories that it carried with it that I was happy to ditch. The garage also stored a gorgeous Austin Healy convertible.

"I've owned this precious thing since the early 70s," he said, gesturing at it with a flourish of pride. "It only comes out for special occasions now, but I make sure it gets a tune-up once a year just to keep it fresh."

"What's that?" I pointed to a large, strange-looking machine in the corner.

"Oh!" Horace exclaimed. "That's the original Echo printing press, back in the days before I went digital. Ah, the smell of fresh ink on paper — takes me back every time. I just don't get the same sensation from my laptop. Ooh, here!" He rummaged around in a box partially hidden behind the printing press. "Have one of these — one of the early print versions of the original magazine. Very rare, you know." He handed it to me and I thanked him distractedly, staring at the rather lurid cover which featured a scantily clad woman cowering in fear as a ghostly figure loomed over her.

"Don't worry," Horace assured me, seeing the way I looked at the magazine. "*The Echo* isn't quite so tawdry these days. The last thing I want is to be mistaken for a tabloid — no pictures of Bigfoot in *The Echo*, you know! Respectability — that's the key to success." He smiled affectionately and patted my arm.

After getting the details, Gareth fired up the truck and trailer and we set out. I was still holding the magazine, rolled up in my hand. "What's that?" Gareth asked as we pulled away.

I laughed. "Just one of Horace's penny dreadfuls." I showed him the cover and he rolled his eyes. "What have we gotten ourselves into?" I shoved the magazine into the pocket behind my seat where it stayed for a very long time.

9

THE CEMETERY ON THE HILL

The case of *Mommy Dearest*, thanks to Horace, gained us quite a bit of notoriety with his readership and earned us our first real fee from poor Harold, who was more than happy to pay it out if it meant his mother could pass on and finally leave him alone. Our relationship with Horace blossomed, leading us to steady employment and an even steadier income. We communicated via email, him sending us requests that he had carefully vetted to ensure they were worthy of a place in *The Echo*, and us sending him back reports that he turned into something a bit more sensational. Terence Kent's sad story became *The Scent of Roses*, Mr. Wiggles was a tongue-in-cheek tale that Horace called *What's New, Pussycat?*, and even little Jenny got a lovely tribute that he titled *The Mystery of the Origami Ghost*. In my reports, I always left out any mention of John Berith, or my search for Harmony

Our most recent assignment from Horace was to rid a cemetery of a ghost. Just one? Although it seems only logical that graveyards would have more than their fare share of spirits, it's the opposite. People are tied to places, and it's the same when they pass—they usually stay somewhere that has meaning to them rather than a cold, lonely cemetery so it's unusual to find a ghost inhabiting one, let alone wreaking havoc from among the tombstones. The cemetery in this case was in Walmot Township, high on a hill overlooking farmers' fields on one side, and a busy new highway on the other. And it was the highway that seemed to be the focus of this particular ghost's attention.

We called the number Horace gave us. It belonged to the Reeve of the township, Reg Symons, who told us the story in a brusque, almost embarrassed way.

"Highway got built. It's a fine highway, despite the protests from the people in town. They're always complaining about something or another. Landfill one week, high speed rail the next, quarries, wind turbines—always a bee in their damn bonnets. Now it's this 'ghost' getting in on the action. They call it The Hilltop Haunt. I don't believe in that bullshit any more than the next guy, but they think it's fantastic. Not so great for all the cars going off the road right by the cemetery though. Not so great for the township either with two lawsuits pending. What I need is for you to go there and see what's going on. If there *is* a ghost, which I highly doubt, get rid of the goddamn thing. If not, well, I guess we'll be spending a lot of money we don't have on regrading and putting up barriers."

When we asked him if he wanted to meet us out there, his immediate response was "No damn way! Just let me know when you're done, whatever happens, and I'll pay you the going rate."

We were coming into Walmot from up North after taking the ferry from Manitoulin into Tobermory. I'd left my charger in the truck while we were onboard and had exhausted my phone battery during the crossing. We had a long drive ahead of us and I was already bored. I was rooting around in the pocket behind my seat, looking for a map, when my hand closed on the magazine Horace had given me ages ago. I pulled it out, that garish cover piquing my interest.

"I'd forgotten all about this," I said to Gareth, flashing the cover at him and grinning. He looked at it out of the corner of his eye and snorted.

"Come on," I entreated him. "It's not like there's anything else to do, and it's going to be a long ride." He sighed in resignation and gave me a quick smile. I opened the magazine—it smelled a little musty after years in Horace's garage and the pages were yellowing. "We're starting at the beginning with...*The Blind River Killer!*" I intoned dramatically. I started to read the stories out loud to Gareth. Unsolved mysteries, ghost sightings, and demonic infestations abounded between the graphically illustrated pages, but we both had to admit that Horace was a solid writer, not too melodramatic, but able to keep the reader in suspense. One story in particular intrigued me. It was about the strange disappearance of a seven-year-old boy, Nicholas Cooper. He and his older brother Mitchell had gone to a local park to play—they were separated and he was never seen again. The brother told the police that he had gone to get them both ice cream, and that Nicholas would never have wandered away on his own. But a witness testified that he had seen Nicholas *and* his brother heading into the forest at the same time that Mitchell insisted he was waiting in line at the snack booth. When I read that, I gasped involuntarily.

"What?" asked Gareth, not taking his eyes off the road.

"It's—do you remember what I told you about Harmony, about the bus driver swearing that he saw me there? He even described what I was wearing. Only it wasn't me. This sounds exactly like that."

"Interesting." It was starting to spit rain so he flicked the wipers on. "We should look into it."

"This magazine is from the seventies. The brother, Mitchell, would be in his early 60s now. I wonder..." I pulled out my phone to see if I could look him up, find out more about the story, but not only was it barely charged, I was also out of data. "Damn. I'll have to wait until we get somewhere with wifi. Don't let me forget."

Gareth nodded and turned the wipers up to high as the rain started to really come down. We sat in silence for a while, listening to the rain pounding the roof of the truck. The radio was playing low and my eyelids were getting heavy. Suddenly, I was in a park. I could hear children's voices, and the sound of music coming from a merry-go-round in the distance. I turned in the direction that the music was coming from and saw a boy running towards me on his way to a wooded area on the other side of the park. He was being followed by a younger boy who was calling out, "Wait up, Mitch!" The older boy kept running ahead as the younger one chased after him, laughing and panting. "Wait for me!"

As the older boy passed in front of me, I yelled, "Hey! Don't leave him behind!" My voice sounded far away and distorted, like it was being mechanically slowed down. The boy stopped and stared at me. He was holding a striped rubber ball that he tossed into the air and caught—once, twice. He paused, then spun and threw it as hard as he could into the woods. He turned back to me and smiled. He looked absolutely normal, ordinary, wearing jeans and a baseball T-shirt with 'Dodgers' written across it, a regular boy. Then his eyes flashed yellow.

"Don't worry, Verity," he said. His voice was happy, prepubescently high-pitched but beneath it there was something low and guttural. "I'll keep him safe. Well, keep him, anyway." He started to laugh, a dark sound that echoed through my mind. Suddenly he stopped and his face grew hard and old. "Go back, hunter. There's nothing for you here. He belongs to me now, like all the rest." He looked over his shoulder as I stood, horrified. "C'mon, Nicky," he yelled, and he took off, the younger boy still in pursuit, still giggling and breathless.

I was frozen in place, my mouth unable to form words. I struggled and strained, and finally, just as they were about to go into the woods, I screamed, "John Berith!" The boy stopped so quickly that the other one, Nicky, almost ran into him. He whispered something to Nicky, who disappeared among the trees. "Give her back to me!" I yelled at the distant figure. "I want Harmony back! Give her back!" I started to sob as the boy in the Dodgers shirt transformed without warning into a man, an ordinary man wearing a non-descript tan jacket. I recognized him right away and my blood froze as his eyes flashed yellow. He opened his mouth and slowly whispered the word "Never." It was carried on the wind to me, multiplying into a horrifying chorus, and when it reached me, I screamed again, a sound made up of loss and despair and fury as he vanished into the woods. All of a sudden, my body jerked. I opened my eyes and saw Gareth gripping the steering wheel, fighting to prevent the truck and trailer from veering off the highway and plunging into the ditch.

"What the hell is going on?" I yelled.

"I could ask you the same thing!" he yelled back, struggling to keep the wheel straight. I could see a hill up ahead, tombstones and memorials jutting up and creating a morbid skyline on its crest. "Screw this!" he growled, and slammed on the brakes. The truck came to an abrupt stop in the middle of the road; luckily, there was no one behind us. Gareth took a deep breath. "We're here," he said calmly. "You were having a bad dream."

"Yes." I stared at the hill up ahead. "I'll tell you about it later. Let's walk the rest of the way."

Gareth drove slowly and carefully onto the shoulder. I stood on the gravel staring at the hilltop graveyard while he got his duffel bag out of the trailer. "There's someone up there," I pointed. A figure was leaning back against the tallest monument, arms crossed leisurely as if waiting, watching the highway below.

Gareth squinted against the sun, the skin around his eyes crinkling. "I don't see anything yet." He shouldered the bag and we walked briskly down the road.

The hill, when we got to it, was steep, and by the time we were halfway up, I was wheezing slightly. Gareth kept climbing, his long legs striding through the tall grass as he made his way to the top. *Wait up, Mitch*, I thought, the dream still lingering like a bad taste in my mouth. I shook it off and caught up to Gareth, breathing hard. When we finally got to the crest, we stopped. I could see the figure in profile. It was a teenaged boy, about fifteen, wearing an ill-fitting black suit jacket, white shirt, long pants with suspenders, and a straw hat. His feet were bare. He was staring intently at the road beneath the hill. A car was approaching, and as it got closer, I saw him wave his hand as if batting away a fly. The car tires squealed and the car began to swerve into the opposite lane. "Hey!!" I called out. He turned, startled. The car below skidded slightly, then corrected its path and continued on.

"You ruined it," he said petulantly. He slammed his fist into the tall granite monument behind him. "Just you wait—I'll get the next one."

"Hmph," Gareth said under his breath. "What do you know? There really is a ghost. And he's a bit of a dick."

"Gareth! He's just a kid!" I hissed. Gareth threw up his hands in the air in mock surrender and put the duffel bag down on the ground.

I addressed the boy. "So, hey. What's your name?"

He stared at me. "You can see me?"

I nodded. His face clouded. "Jacob Entz. But it doesn't matter. Stuck here in this godforsaken place by myself. At least it used to be quiet. But these roaring machines are so annoying—I *hate* them! The next one is going in the ditch and you can't stop me!"

In the distance, I could hear vehicles approaching. As they got closer, I realized it was a large transport truck in one direction and an SUV coming from the other. If he was able to make even one of them go into the other's lane, it could mean potential death for everyone involved. Trying to keep the desperation out of my voice, I said, "Jacob, look at me. Maybe we can help you. You're not the first person who's gone through this, and my partner and I know what to do." His hand was in mid-air, ready to make the sweeping motion that would cause chaos. I didn't know how else to distract him so I blurted out, "You're really cute—do you have a girlfriend?"

It worked. His head whipped around and his hand stopped in mid-air. I thought for a minute that he would be boastful, swagger a little maybe, but instead, his eyes filled with tears.

"I had a sweetheart once." His voice was choked with emotion. "Her name was Celeste. I don't know where she is now. It's so unfair! Is it because of what I did? I'm sorry, all right? Can I please just go home?" He wiped the tears off his face roughly and sank to the ground. The truck and SUV mercifully passed by each other, unaware of how close they had both come to disaster.

"Where's home?" I asked quietly. Without looking up, he pointed at a farmhouse in the distance. It was a large red brick home with an unusual key-shaped window partway up. There was a large barn out back and, without the noise of traffic, I could hear cattle lowing from the field beyond it. "It's beautiful," I said. "Very peaceful."

His face flushed with anger. "It was until all the machines came. I hate them, hate their roaring!"

I gave Gareth a pointed look. He bent down to get the box out of the duffel bag. "What if I told you that you could see Celeste again?" I asked. I had no idea if it was true—who knew how long he'd been here, existing in a half-life until the highway construction had awakened him.

He looked doubtful. "I don't believe you. He told me all about the box, about how it would take me to somewhere called 'Oblivion' because of...because of my mistake.

He said 'Jacob, if they come, don't listen. Make sure you never leave."

"Who's 'he'?" I asked, but I was pretty sure I already knew the answer.

"My friend John. My *only* friend. And I don't want to go to 'Oblivion', wherever that is, so you can—" his voice became louder and more strident as he started to walk towards us very deliberately, fists clenched, "—you can *go to hell*!!"

"Jacob," I said in a deceptively calm voice, backing away as he got dangerously close to us. "Why don't you let us explain about the box, and then you can decide what you want to do. Gareth, can you tell Jacob about the box?"

Gareth, picking up on my cue, said, "Sure, Verity. I can tell Jacob about the box." He held it up in front of himself in one hand. With the other hand, he traced the carvings as he spoke, his voice hypnotic and soothing. "The box is a symbol of passage," he intoned, focusing on the swirls and insignias. "When the lid is open, it signals possibility. When the lid is closed, you're finally home. This world has nothing for you anymore. The world beyond the box contains the energy of everyone you've ever loved, everyone who has gone before you and after you. When you decide to go into the box, you embrace a future that is more joyful than your present existence. I hold the box. I hold the conduit to peace, to a pure existence of light and love. The decision is yours."

Jacob's face was a portrait of conflict and torment. "I want to go, but John—"

In the distance, another vehicle was drawing close. Jacob turned but I said quickly, "The box, Jacob. John was wrong. There's no Oblivion; there's only peace. It's so quiet on the other side. Wouldn't you like that?" He looked at me, his face full of grief.

"I would," he said. "I hate it here. I want—" He reached out his hand towards the box. Gareth held it up, steady, reassuring. Riveted by the box, watching his hand move towards it almost involuntarily, getting closer and closer, Jacob spoke one last time. "John said to give you a message. He said that Harmony—" With that, he suddenly disappeared.

"Harmony WHAT?!" I shrieked as he vanished from sight. I stared at Gareth, my eyes wide with shock. "What was he going to say?! Why did you let him go in?!!"

Gareth looked grieved. "I'm sorry," he said. "I didn't realize he was so close."

I fell to the ground and huddled next to one of the tombstones, holding my head in my hands, trying not to cry hysterically. I knew on a rational level that it wasn't Gareth's fault, but being so close to some knowledge about Harmony and then having that snatched away...it was more than I could bear, and I let it all go.

Gareth leaned down and put his hand gently on my shoulder as I heaved with sobs. After what seemed like forever, I reached up and put my hand over his. "I'm all right." He helped me up and I used my sleeve to wipe the last of the tears away.

"What do you want to do now?" he asked, concerned.

I squeezed his hand and then let it go. "Now?" I said. "Now we find Mitchell Cooper."

10

MITCHELL COOPER

We weren't five minutes down the road when a grinding sound started coming from the trailer. "We have a problem," Gareth said sourly. "All that swerving must have damaged something." We pulled over onto the shoulder and after crouching down and shining a flashlight into the truck bed, Gareth straightened up. "Damn kid. Hitch is bent. We can't keep driving like this."

We decided the best course of action was to head to the township office and talk to the Reeve. Gareth reluctantly unhooked the trailer and locked it up tight. "At least no one can drive away with it like this," I reassured him. He looked more perturbed than I'd seen him in a long time. He could easily face down a malevolent or help a spirit cross over, but the trailer was sacrosanct. It had been his home for more years that I knew — my home now too — and he was very attached to it, attached to the faded carpeting, 1970s pine cupboards, the shower with terrible water pressure, and especially the lumpy tweed pull-out sofa where he slept at night so that I could have the bed. He'd left home as soon as he'd finished high school, he told me once, and he'd bought his first truck and this fifth wheel not long after. He'd had other trucks since then, but the trailer was the one constant in his life.

The time in between him setting out on his own and meeting me in Kincardine was a mystery. Gareth didn't talk much about anything, let alone himself, unless he was very drunk, so I'd pieced together a lot of his history and filled in the rest with speculation. I knew that he'd gone to university and majored in philosophy but hadn't finished his degree for reasons that he refused to divulge. I knew that he had worked as a bartender, on the line in a car factory, hotel night shift manager, and a variety of other jobs that let him pay the bills and pursue his other 'interests'. I knew that like me, he was estranged from his parents and that when his father died, he hadn't gone to the funeral. And I knew that his guilt over Julia still haunted him, and that sometimes he would cry out her name in his sleep. All this, but I didn't really know him at all; the only two things I was really sure about were first, that he loved that trailer, and second, that I could trust him. Which I did, completely.

We pulled into the township office close to 4 o'clock, hoping to catch the Reeve before he went home.

"You're in luck!" exclaimed the perky, elderly woman behind the reception desk. Reading glasses hung from a chain around her neck. She put them on, picked up the receiver of an old multi-line phone and carefully punched in five digits. "Mr. Symons," she announced cheerily, "you have a couple of visitors…yes…no…I understand." She put down the receiver, still smiling, but this time the smile was strained. "Gosh. I'm so sorry but Mr. Symons was just on his way out. He says, 'Why don't you give him a call tomorrow?" As she was speaking, we saw a figure through the frosted glass that separated her from the offices. It was moving quickly, heading towards an exit sign. Gareth turned on his heel and took off down the stairs into the parking lot.

"Uh, have a nice day!" I called out to her, right behind Gareth. When I got to the bottom of the stairs, Gareth was already in the parking lot, walking quickly to intercept the man who'd come out of the back exit. I hurried to catch up as Gareth yelled, "Hey there! Mr. Symons!" The man turned and hesitated. He was short and wide, his ample stomach spilling over his belt. His hair was grey and thinning, and he twitched nervously as Gareth strode towards him, his long legs quickly closing the gap between him and his target.

"Oh, hello there," the Reeve addressed him, with forced courtesy. His eyes were darting back and forth, looking for an escape. "Mr. Winter, is it?"

"Yes," Gareth answered. He said nothing else.

The silence was becoming uncomfortable as the two men stared at each other, so as I approached them, I called out, "Mr. Symons! We don't mean to bother you but we were hoping to discuss the cemetery and our payment. We—"

"Keep it down!" he hissed. "I'd really prefer this stayed under wraps. Can you imagine what would happen if the town council knew I'd hired a couple of—of ghostbusters?"

"Sorry," I said in a low voice. "We just wanted to give you our report. Also, we've had a few unexpected expenses that we need to come to an agreement about."

His face became stormy. "I knew it! Trying to con me out of even more money! Well, if you think—"

Gareth interrupted. He sounded calm but I could tell he was furious. "Actually, if *you* think you can stand here and insult us after we fulfilled our end of the contract, got rid of your ghost and any future lawsuits, and ended up with a damaged vehicle, then maybe the town council *will* find out about us."

The Reeve put his hands up in protest. "All right, all right," he blustered. "But how do I know there really *was* a ghost? Can you prove it?"

"His name was Jacob Entz," I said quietly. "He was about 15, said he'd lived in the house at the bottom of the hill, the one with the key-shaped window. He'd been attached to the cemetery for a long time, but the highway construction made him manifest. We looked but couldn't find any grave markers with his name on them."

"Jacob Entz, was it? All right. Let's go back in and take a look at the records, see if we can't verify your ghost. If we can, then I'll pay you what I owe you. If not...." His unspoken threat hung in the air.

Gareth gestured. "After you."

We followed Mr. Symons back into the township building. "I'm just here for a few minutes, Gloria," he said to the receptionist, who looked surprised to see us all back. "You can go home now if you'd like." She thanked him and started packing up, watching us with curiosity as he took us into his office. "All our records are computerized now," he said. "Shouldn't take a minute." We sat silently while he focused on the screen in front of him, clicking and typing. Suddenly his face went pale.

"Well, I know why you didn't find his grave marker. 'Jacob Entz, 1893: By his own hand'. If he'd committed suicide, he wouldn't have been allowed to be buried in the cemetery. There's an area just outside the cemetery proper that's considered unhallowed ground. He would have been put there." He sighed. "There's no way you could have known that unless you'd...talked to him. I guess I owe you an apology."

"You owe us five hundred dollars for crossing him over," Gareth said bluntly. "Plus repairs to our vehicle. Your ghost bent my fifth-wheel hitch."

Without argument, the Reeve wrote us a cheque for our fee. "I'll have your fifth wheel towed to my cousin's garage just up the road in Festival City. I'll call ahead to them and have the repairs billed to me. Might take a couple of days, so here's the address of a great hotel—I'll cover that too. And it's theatre season right how, so if you like Shakespeare, you can take in a show or two. Let me know if you want any tickets." He sighed again. "I never really believed in ghosts before—I thought this whole thing was just a prank, or more bullshit from the community group. But now…I suppose I have to rethink everything."

"I suppose you do." Gareth put the cheque in his shirt pocket and we left Mr. Symons sitting at his desk, staring into space.

By the time Gareth and I drove back to meet the tow truck driver, saw the fifth wheel safely hoisted up and on its way, and then drove to the hotel, we were both exhausted. And after relating my nightmare to Gareth on the way to Festival City, seeing a show was the last thing on my mind. The first thing was to get into the hotel room, finish charging my phone and hook into the free wifi. While Gareth napped in his room next door before dinner, I had a phone call to make.

Horace was elated to hear from me, if his voice on the other end of the line was any indication. "My dear Miss Darkwood, how *are* you?" he asked. "Do you have anything interesting to report about your latest adventure? I already have a working title— "Ghostly Road Rage". What do you think?"

I reassured Horace that our report would be coming in the morning, then got to the point. "Horace, do you remember that issue of *The Echo* you gave me when we first met? There was a story in it called '*The Dodger Doppelganger*'."

"How could I forget?" Horace sighed. "Tragic case. The little boy was never found."

"Do you happen to know what happened to the older brother? The one who said he was getting ice cream when the younger boy disappeared?"

Horace pondered for a moment. "Hmm. I seem to vaguely remember hearing something about him. Hang on a minute." There was the sound of file drawers opening and closing, the rustle of paper, then Horace was back. "Yes, I was right. There was an inquest about 6 years later when the case was finally closed, and the young man had a breakdown right after. It was in all the papers, people assuming it was because he was guilty even though he denied it to the bitter end. I never believed he was involved, of course. There's a lot of evidence to support the existence of doppelgangers. For instance—"

"Horace," I hated to interrupt him, but I knew how difficult it was to get Horace back on track once he went on a tangent. "Do you know where Mitchell Cooper is right now? Is he still alive? I need to talk to him about something."

"You do?" Horace's interest was piqued and his voice became conspiratorial. "Sounds delicious. How can I help?"

Horace was more than happy to reach out to what he called his "spiritual connections". I didn't ask if they were corporeal or not; I was too anxious. I paced the room for a bit, then scolded myself for my impatience. Horace was a magazine editor, not a miracle worker, and it might be days before he was able to dig anything up on Mitchell Cooper. I forced myself to sit down and focus on the report I'd promised Horace. Normally, I had no trouble writing about the events of an assignment, but this time it was difficult. I didn't know if it was because I had so much empathy for Jacob, and how miserable he must have been to have died 'by his own hand', or if it was because I was so distracted by Mitchell Cooper and the possibility of a lead into Harmony's disappearance. I was finally putting the finishing touches on the report when there was a knock on my door.

"I've found something interesting." Gareth had his laptop tucked under his arm. His calm demeanour belied his excitement but I could tell; his hair was slightly disheveled from his earlier nap and he hadn't bothered to comb it back down.

"About Mitchell Cooper?"

"No, John Berith." He put his laptop down on the bed and opened it. "It's a very uncommon name," he said, clicking on a link. "The only references I could find, aside from that minor Biblical reference and characters named Berith in computer games, are on a subthread of this website. It's called *Perchance to Dream*. The subthread is people who've had prophetic dreams that they claim later came true. Look at this one."

We both read a post from a user called ISeeDeadPeople, claiming that she'd had a dream about her grandmother, who had warned that "John Berith was in the neighbourhood" and to be careful. About a week later, the 6-year-old son of a family down the street had gone missing. "I was eight when my grandmother came to me," ISeeDeadPeople claimed. "I'd never seen her spirit before and haven't since. I barely knew her before she died, but there she was, just as I remembered her, telling me to be careful. I was terrified for days, thinking that this John Berith was the boogeyman under my bed. Turns out it wasn't *my* bed he was under."

"There are comments on this post," Gareth said, scrolling down. "See? This one talks about John Berith appearing in a dream to his dad in the nineteen forties."

"Who—or what is he?"

Gareth shrugged. "All the descriptions of him are the same. 'The most ordinary-looking man I'd ever seen', 'a regular fellow', 'non-descript'—it's the same man I dreamed about as a boy."

"And the same one Uncle Pat warned us about." I was about to ask Gareth if any of the stories talked about the man having yellow eyes when the phone rang. I leapt for it. Horace's voice on the other end was a relief. "That was quick!" I exclaimed, letting my enthusiasm get the better of me. "It's Horace," I whispered to Gareth. "I asked him to look into Mitchell Cooper."

The call with Horace was short and sweet. He'd located Mitchell Cooper, now in his sixties, in Halifax. "I have a contact number for him," Horace said, obviously pleased with himself. "You *will* fill me in on the details later? What a marvellous addendum to the original story. It's given me the most wonderful idea for a *'Where Are They Now?'* series! By the way, if you're heading towards Halifax, you could do me a huge favour and stop off in one of the Quebec parishes. Seems there's a church with a very persistent demon that needs exorcising—the local priest is at his wit's end!"

Gareth and I agreed, me very reluctantly, to the detour. We said our goodbyes to Horace, promising to keep him up to date. As soon as we hung up, I immediately dialed the Halifax number Horace had given us for Mitchell Cooper. I waited breathlessly as it rang and rang. Finally someone picked up.

"Hello," a quiet voice said.

I paused, not sure how he would react, how best to frame my request. But I didn't need to worry. "Mr. Cooper," I started, "my name is Verity Darkwood."

"Verity Darkwood," the voice on the other end of the phone exhaled heavily. "I was wondering when I would hear from you."

II

THE SEVENTH DEVIL

The conversation with Mitchell Cooper was surreal. When I asked how he knew I'd be calling him, he said, "I dreamed about you."

Mitchell Cooper had had the same terrible recurring dream for the past fifty years. In it, he saw his little brother Nicky as clear as day. He also saw himself. But he knew it wasn't himself that he was watching—he was looking at the creature, or whatever it was, who stole Nicky away from him and his parents. At least three nights a week, he stood helpless, as Nicky ran past him after another boy, identical to Mitchell in every way. And just as he disappeared into the woods, never to be seen again, the other Mitchell would stop, slowly turn with a terrible smile and say, "I'll keep him safe. Well, keep him, anyway." He could have numbed himself, gotten drunk every night, or taken drugs to let him sleep dreamlessly, but he wouldn't. It was the only way he could see his little brother, catch that one last glimpse of him before he was gone forever. The dream was always heartbreaking, and always the same, until a week ago when things changed.

"Changed how?" I asked.

"This time there was someone else watching, someone I'm assuming was you. The other Mitchell said your name: 'Don't worry, Verity.' It's not a common name so when you called, I assumed it was you. You were standing by the woods when they ran past you. You've been there every night this week, just watching, and then last night, you spoke to him and he answered."

"I don't understand," I said. "I had the same dream, but I've only had it once—this afternoon. At least I think it was only once." *Had* I dreamed it before? I wasn't so sure now—I was getting flashes of it, mixed in with other dreams, the ones I had about Harmony.

"I'm not sure what to tell you. You've been there in the park every night for a week, silent until last night. Then, after he spoke to you, you screamed the name 'John Berith'. Who's John Berith?"

"That's a long story. Look, my partner and I are heading out your way—we have a stop in Quebec, but then we'll come to you. I'll explain everything, at least what I understand, when we meet."

He was reluctant to hang up, as if when the conversation ended, I would vanish like his brother, but I reassured him that we would be there as soon as we could, and hopefully have even more information to share with him.

Gareth and I ordered Chinese take-out and had it delivered to his room. We sat eating in comfortable silence, then I had a sudden thought. "Do you think Horace might be able to do a little research, see if there are any other unsolved disappearances involving doppelgangers, anything weird like that?"

Gareth cracked open a fortune cookie. "Hmm. 'A hunch is creativity trying to tell you something'. According to this fortune cookie, contacting Horace is a good idea."

"You're not supposed to choose your own fortune cookie," I said, taking it from him and biting into it. "I'll call Horace when we've cleaned up. The cookie has spoken."

Gareth snorted. "Don't put too much stock in something manufactured in a factory overseas. It's the same advice hundreds of people get every day. Just as bad as horoscopes."

"I'm a Cancer," I winked at him. "Some people really believe in astrology, you know."

"And I'm a Taurus, one in a million. Or several million. People believe in a lot of things. God, Jehovah, Buddha, heaven, hell, reincarnation, nirvana—I walked the Noble Eightfold Path myself once. Quit before I got to the end."

"Why?" I asked, trying to sound nonchalant. Gareth's past was enigmatic, and I was secretly excited whenever he seemed inclined to share more about it.

"I'd learned everything I wanted to know. Same with the seminary—got what I needed and left before they could ordain me."

"You said you never finished your philosophy degree either."

"Life's a journey, not a destination. There's only one thing in this life that I've ever cared to finish, and I think you know what that is."

I nodded. He'd never come out and actually told me, but I instinctively knew that he was talking about Julia, about finding out what had happened to her.

"People can believe whatever they want," he continued, cracking open the fortune cookie I'd handed him and throwing the tiny slip of paper into the garbage without looking at it. "Maybe some or all or even none of it is true. It's not my place to say or to judge. The only thing I know for certain is that evil exists. I've seen it with my own two eyes."

"I've seen it too," I agreed. "So has Mitchell Cooper. And who knows how many other people."

I placed the empty food containers in a plastic bag, tied it tight and went to put it in the garbage can. Gareth's fortune lay there, face up. It said, "You only treasure what you have lost." I pretended not to see it and sat back down on the bed.

"Let me know what Horace says." Gareth yawned. "I'm having an early night. See you bright and early if we want to pick up the trailer and get on the road to the Eastern townships."

I went back to my room and called Horace. After several rings, he answered. And from the background noise, it sounded like he was having a party.

"I'm so sorry to interrupt," I said. "I can call back tomorrow."

"No, my dear, it's perfectly all right. I'm just hosting a small soiree!" He moved the phone away from his mouth and called out, "Don't start the séance without me!" Then he was back, laughing breathlessly.

When I told him what we needed, he was thrilled. "You know I love a good doppelganger! Give me a little time — I'll see what I can find." As I was hanging up, I heard him yelling, "Marcus, where did you put the Ouija board?" and then he was gone. I smiled to myself. Horace was certainly unconventional but I had no doubt he would find us the information we needed if it was out there.

In the morning, Gareth was true to his word, knocking on my door at 7 am. "The garage opens at 8. Just enough time to get ready for the day, grab some breakfast, and be on our way."

I took the first driving shift. The trip would take at least eight hours, not counting stops for lunch, leg stretches, and bathroom breaks. Gareth opened the laptop and grabbed my phone. I looked at him out of the corner of my eye. "Don't worry," he said. "The fee for the last job will cover the data charges — the Reeve kicked in a little extra. I need to do some research."

"What are you looking for?"

"Just following up with those posts on the *Perchance To Dream* website. I think I told you before that the only Berith I was familiar with was a demon from the Old Testament. I want to dig a bit more."

I pulled onto the 401 and settled into the right lane with the cruise control set to slightly over the speed limit. I wasn't a fan of highway driving under any circumstances, but especially not while hauling a fifth wheel. Still, it was only fair that we take turns, and maybe Gareth would find something important that would help us figure out who John Berith was, and how to find him. After half an hour, Gareth said, "OK, this is interesting. In 1653, a French priest named Dominic Carreau wrote a book called *The Seventh Devil*, which included a classification of demons. According to Carreau, who was a renowned exorcist, a demon named Berith appeared to him while he was exorcising a nun and told him about the different hierarchies of demons. There are seven demons in the first hierarchy and Berith is supposedly one of them. Carreau described the demon Berith as 'like the common man in visage'. He refers to Berith in a poem he wrote—here's the translation:

There's the devil you know and the devil you don't,
the devil you'll meet and the devil you won't,
a devil that's tall and a devil that's small,
and a devil that's human after all.

"So John Berith is the Seventh Devil? A devil who's human? How is that possible?" I asked.

Gareth paused in thought for a moment. "It makes sense when you think about it. There are stories going back to the forties, maybe even further, that mention the 'ordinary man'; they all describe him exactly the way that Carreau does. Maybe it's a malevolent—a really powerful one—that can inhabit a man and control his actions without raising suspicion, but who can also appear in human form as well as its own on other planes. Remember what Jenny said about the man who wanted her to go with him?"

"She called him Oni. He was wearing a devil mask, and when he took it off, he looked like a regular man, like the 'bad men' who forced her family to go to a labour camp."

"Says here an Oni is a Japanese demon," Gareth said, scrolling through a website. "Interesting. Malevolents are usually pretty localized—they don't normally stray too far from one belief system. They depend too much on people's willingness to entertain their existence, and they're not known for their intelligence. If this John Berith *is* some kind of malevolent, he's different than anything we've encountered. Especially if he can manifest in dreams."

I shivered. The thought that John Berith, whoever or whatever he may be, could walk through my dreams whenever he pleased made the insomnia that plagued me sound like the better option. Gareth went back to his research and we continued down the highway. Once we crossed the border into Quebec, we switched and Gareth took the wheel while I relaxed. Or at least tried to. My mind was racing with questions. If John Berith *was* some kind of super-malevolent, why would he have taken Harmony? And what had he done with her? Was she still alive? I'd given up hope of that years ago, not being able to bear the torturous thought that she might still be out there, suffering at the hands of whoever had stolen her. Better to believe she was dead. But this? To be dead and still forced to exist in a half-life with the likes of John Berith...a scream began forming in my throat, and I started to shake. Gareth gave me a quick look and immediately changed lanes to pull off the road. He'd seen me like this before, on the edge of a full-blown panic attack, and knew it was going to get worse before it got better if he didn't intervene. He threw the truck into park and hurried around to the passenger side, opening my door and taking me by the shoulders.

"Look at me," he ordered. "Breathe. In through the nose—1, 2, 3, 4, 5. Out through the mouth—1, 2, 3, 4, 5." He reached into his pocket and pulled out a coin. "Focus on this. What year was it minted?"

I tried to concentrate on the coin. It was a silver dollar—real silver, not made of nickel like they are now. "1967," I said shakily.

"Good. How much is it worth?"

"One dollar."

Gareth laughed. "More than that. With the right buyer, I could get a hundred for it, maybe more. What's on it?"

I squinted at the coin. I could feel my heart slowing down, my breathing steadying. "It looks like a very large bird. Goose?"

"Goose it is." Gareth put the coin back in his pocket. "We good?"

I nodded, still trying to breathe slowly and deliberately. "You haven't had one of those for a while," he said. "Why didn't you tell me things were getting bad again?"

"They weren't particularly. It just came over me suddenly. I'm okay now, thanks."

"Do you want to talk about it?"

I shook my head. "Maybe later but not right now. I don't want to trigger another one. How far away are we?"

"We're getting close—another couple of hours," Gareth eased the truck and trailer back into traffic. "While you were driving, I messaged Horace and asked him to contact the priest, a Father Paradis, let him know that we'd be there around 6 pm. He also made reservations for us at a campsite about ten minutes outside of Saint-Cecile. I'd rather get the job done before we settle in for the night, and be on our way in the morning."

I nodded in agreement. I was anxious to get to Halifax and meet Mitchell Cooper, and we were still at least two days away from him, with a demonic exorcism between now and then.

12

LE DIABLE DE SAINT-CECILE

We pulled into Saint-Cecile around 6 o'clock as promised. It was a sleepy little village, with a population of around five hundred people. There were a couple of cute cafés, and a general store with tourists mingling around outside on the patio.

"Quaint," Gareth pronounced. We made our way up the road to the church where Father Paradis was waiting. It was a pretty church, not as large as I'd expected, red brick with a tall white steeple, and imposing wooden double doors. The only thing that really set it apart was the windows. I assumed they would be stained glass, probably depictions of events from the Bible, but no one would be able to tell right now—they were covered in some kind of black substance. Gareth parked and we got out of the truck. I stood for a minute on the sidewalk leading up to the double doors, scrutinizing the building while I waited for Gareth to get the duffel bag out of the trailer.

"Is that paint?" I asked as he came up behind me.

"Looks thicker than paint." Gareth craned his neck to look at the windows set into the steeple. "Tar? Some kind of resin?" He curled his lip in distaste, and looked around. "Do you feel anything yet?"

I was just about to answer when the double doors flew open and a man came rushing out. He was wearing a cassock and priest's collar, and he clutched a large crucifix in his hand. "T'ank da 'oly Father that you're 'ere!" he exclaimed in a heavily accented voice. His face was red with effort, and smudged with what looked like the same black substance as the windows. "It's getting worse, and I can't stop it!" He gestured wildly at the open doors. "Come quickly! Vite, vite!" He gestured again, half-walking, half-running backwards towards the church entrance. Gareth shouldered his duffel bag and we followed Father Paradis into the foyer.

The interior of the church was shocking. The black gunk that covered the windows also dripped from the pews, covered the floor and walls, and was splashed over the statues of the Virgin Mary and other saints I didn't recognize. The smell was disgusting—a combination of feces and garbage. I gagged involuntarily and Gareth covered his mouth and nose with the inside of his elbow.

"What *is* that?!" I exclaimed, my eyes watering. "Is it sewage?"

The priest replied, "Non! It's sheet."

"Sheets of what?" asked Gareth, coughing.

"Sheet!" Father Paradis repeated. "La merde!"

I looked down at my shoes and grimaced. We were standing in a pool of the vile stuff, and it was spreading, almost as if it had a will of its own, towards the door, threatening to spill out over the sill and make its way into the village.

Father Paradis was almost in tears. He started waving his crucifix around and yelled something in Latin. "Exorcizamus te, omnis immundus spiritus, omnis satanica potestas—"

"That's not going to help," Gareth interrupted. The priest stopped and stared wide-eyed at Gareth in despair.

"Look...Father...why don't you go to that nice café downtown and let us deal with this?"

Father Paradis hesitated for a moment, caught between his love of the church he was trying to protect and the terror that he was feeling. Finally, he acquiesced. "D'accord," he said. "'Orace said you could be trusted. I will be at le petit café on rue Miquelon." With that, he hurried away, holding his cassock up around his knees so that the hem wouldn't get covered in filth.

Gareth and I stood in the stillness of the church, listening to the steady dripping of excrement as it fell from the domed ceiling onto the altar like black rain. I could sense a presence—the air seemed to be pulsing and the walls of the church expanded and contracted in time with it, as if the building itself was alive. Gareth silently tapped me on the shoulder and pointed to a giant crucifix hanging on the wall behind the altar. The figure of Jesus was the only thing in the entire church that wasn't covered in black waste—in fact, it was pristine. The head of the statue was hanging down, but as we walked towards it, our feet squelching in the mess on the floor, I realized its eyes, which seemed to be downcast as well, were watching us, and the mouth was slightly upturned at one corner in amusement. It was unsettling, to say the least, but when we were standing right underneath it, the head swivelled towards us and its face changed from benevolent to...well, malevolent. A guttural laugh exploded from the mouth of the statue and echoed throughout the church. More liquid excrement rained down from the ceiling onto the altar.

Gareth rolled his eyes, pulled a couple of umbrellas out of his bag, and handed one to me. We opened them up just as the drops reached us. "The shit's a nice touch, but give it a rest. We need to talk."

The laughter stopped abruptly and the statue spoke. "Who seeks an audience with Lutin?" it demanded.

"You're a lutin?" Gareth asked. "Interesting."

"Not *a* lutin!" the statue proclaimed petulantly. "*The* Lutin!"

"What the hell is a 'lutin'?" I whispered.

Gareth answered, sotto voce. "It's a minor malevolent, like an imp. Nasty, not very bright. And definitely lacking in personal hygiene." He raised his voice to address the lutin. "What do you want here? Or are you just having fun?"

The statue cackled. "Fun, yes! Watching the cross-man cry and yell the old words is fun. He thinks he can banish me back to the dark with all his magic talk but I know better. I like it here. So very warm and quiet now that the cross-man and his people are all gone! Many lovely treasures."

"You can't stay here," I said. "You have to go back to where you came from and leave Father Paradis and his congregation alone."

"NOOO!!" the statue roared. "I will not go!"

Gareth opened up the duffel bag. The statue watched him suspiciously as he took out the jar of salt, another jar full of white rice, and placed them on the pew next to him. Then he took out a small vial. When it saw the vial, the lutin started laughing maniacally. "Salt and holy water," it said gleefully. "Such things cannot harm Lutin."

"Who said this was holy water?" Gareth replied, casually uncapping the vial. The statue looked uncertain. "Did you know," Gareth continued, "that when you mix vinegar—" he flourished the vial, "—and salt together, it creates something called 'hydrochloric acid'? Great for cleaning pennies and wonderful for cleansing buildings of malevolents like you."

The statue's eyes widened and the lutin began to struggle within the figure of Christ on the crucifix, whipping its head back and forth. "No!" it screamed, and the black rain came down harder, the smell of excrement filling my nostrils and making me want to retch.

Suddenly I had an idea. "Stop! What about a deal?"

The lutin stopped struggling and looked at me curiously. "What is 'deal'?" it asked, its interest obviously piqued.

"Let's make a bargain. We give you a treasure of your own, and you answer some questions. Then you go."

The statue's eyes narrowed. "What kind of treasure?"

"Gareth," I said, "show Lutin the treasure."

Gareth looked at me blankly. "What treasure?"

I whispered, "The silver dollar. Give it the silver dollar you have in your pocket."

Gareth protested. "But that's worth—"

"A lot of information maybe," I finished his statement. "Come on! I'll get you another one later."

Gareth shook his head in disbelief but pulled the silver dollar out of his pocket and held it up. The lutin's eyes widened and suddenly, it came leaping out of the statue. It was small and red, shaped kind of like a Capuchin monkey but with horns and pointed ears. It gambolled up to Gareth and snatched the silver dollar from his hand. "Pretty!" it cooed, turning the coin from one side to another and watching the way it caught the light.

"OK," I said. "You have a shiny treasure. Now you answer questions."

The lutin was fixated by the coin. "Funny bird," it murmured, stroking the image of the goose.

Gareth and I watched it for a minute. "Not sure how much it knows, or whether it can focus long enough to even tell you," he said. "I hope it's worth the effort—and my coin."

I decided to get right to the point. "Lutin?" I asked in a sweet voice. It didn't look at me; it just kept twirling the coin between its fingers and thumbs and laughing softly. "Lutin!" I called more forcefully. It stopped what it was doing and stared at me. "Do you know who John Berith is?"

The lutin stroked the coin against its cheek and sighed lovingly. "John Berith you do not want to know. He is the Seventh but not the least. He goes by many names. He is Apep and Barong and Jinn and Suanggi and many more. He is older than time and is the eater of souls. He is king of the half-light; he walks among men unseen. He travels with a child always." It threw the coin in the air and caught it. "John Berith you do not want to know," it repeated solemnly.

"He travels with a child always?" I repeated. "Why?"

The lutin continued staring at the coin and said absently, "The souls of children have the most pure energy. John Berith is older than time. This treasure will light up the darkness. Mmm." It started to phase out of existence into its own plane, but Gareth yelled, "Wait a minute!" The lutin paused. "You can't leave the church like this. It's filthy. Clean it up."

It regarded Gareth imperiously. "You, command the great Lutin? Use words of supplication and your wishes might be considered."

Gareth glared daggers at the creature. "Fine," he said, gritting his teeth. "*Please* clean it up."

The lutin giggled. It kissed the coin and snapped its fingers. As it began to fade away, so too did the pools of excrement and the splashes of 'merde' on the pews and walls. The stained-glass windows slowly reappeared from beneath the sludge, their images bright with light from the setting sun gleaming across the altar, which was now immaculate. The Christ on the cross against the back wall resumed his benevolent gaze. I sagged against a pew with my head in my hands, exhausted and full of anguish.

"What did the lutin mean?" I asked Gareth weakly. "'He travels with children and eats their souls'?"

"I've heard of something like that before. Evil forces that sustain themselves with the energy of other beings, like the Langsuir or the Dzoavits."

"So there's no hope then." I could feel my eyes filling up with tears. "What's the point? Of any of this!"

"Don't say that," Gareth said softly. "If John Berith does have her, the point is that we need to save her, help her move on, and stop him from doing it to any other child. He's been stealing them for a long time, and it's up to us to make sure no other sister or brother or mother or father loses someone they love. Do you really want to leave Harmony with him until he's used her all up?"

"Of course not!" I was sobbing for real now, overcome by the knowledge that I would never get over the guilt, that I'd lost her in the worst way possible, and that it would never *not* be my fault.

"Then get up," he said firmly. "Get up and keep going. We have a long road ahead of us, and the waterworks aren't doing anyone any good. Come on." With that, he walked out of the church. I knew he was right. He'd suffered too, for a lot longer than I had. I wiped my eyes with the heel of my palm and did as Gareth ordered. He was putting the duffel bag away as I approached. He turned to face me with a pained expression.

"I didn't mean to—"

"Don't apologize. You're right. There's more at stake than my loss—or yours. I could use a walk. Do you want to go find Father Paradis? Then we can be on our way."

The priest was sitting woefully in the corner of a charming café, staring into a teacup. While Gareth attempted to order us coffee and sandwiches using his long-forgotten high school French, I sat down at the table with Father Paradis. He looked haggard. I put my hand on top of his and said quietly, "It's over. The...demon is gone and the church is fine."

His eyes opened wide and he hugged his crucifix against his chest. "No more sheet?" he asked.

"No more merde," I answered. He crossed himself in relief and said something in Latin. Gareth arrived with the coffee and sandwiches as Father Paradis was excusing himself.

"I must see it with my own eyes and feel da peace of da sanctuary. I will send you le tranfert electronique!" and with that, he hurried out.

Gareth laughed. "Exorcising demons for electronic cash—changed days, indeed. Eat up—we need to be on the road bright and early again. It's a long way to Halifax."

I finished my sandwich, and silently prayed for a dreamless sleep.

13

HALIFAX PART ONE

The campground was quiet, but despite that, I was awake most of the night—a combination of nervous energy and fear that if I closed my eyes for too long, I would be plunged back into nightmares. I was ready to see John Berith again, but prepared and on my own terms, which meant gathering more information. And for that, I needed Horace, as well as Mitchell Cooper.

There was a small supply store on site, and I was able to score some cereal and milk. I got back and Gareth was already awake too, tidying things up so that we could get on the road.

"Look," I said, putting a set of assorted tiny cereal boxes on the counter. "I got us a 'Fun Pak'."

Gareth gave the cereal a skeptical glance. "It doesn't look like fun to me."

"Come on," I laughed. "Have some Frooty Loops."

"I'll take the ones shaped like chocolate donuts," he said dourly, pouring them into a bowl.

We ate quickly and left Saint-Cecile behind. Gareth took the first shift as we made our way towards the New

Brunswick border, skirting along the St. Lawrence River. There were two routes we could have taken, but even though the other was slightly faster, it would have forced us to travel through Maine, and I didn't have a passport. We'd never gone anywhere as a family, let alone into the States, so I'd never needed one. Family holidays weren't something my mother was interested in when it was just her, dad, and me, although she had promised Harmony that when she was older, we would all go to Disneyland. Sometimes it occurred to me that if I hadn't been so selfish, if I'd been at the bus stop on time, we'd be there right now, like in a parallel universe where she's twelve and I'm in university maybe, and as a present to both of us, we're at Disney, riding Space Mountain and shaking Mickey's hand. I can see her as clear as day: taller, long hair pulled back in a high ponytail with blonde tendrils escaping and curling around her face. There she is, laughing shyly as Mickey asks her name. "Harmony," she says, looking at me with a smile. "And this is my sister Veevee."

Then it all fades and I'm left with nothing.

I shoved the grief angrily behind a door in my mind and locked it away. If John Berith was the one who stole her and ruined my life, he'd get what was coming to him if it was the last thing I ever did. I shook off the emotions and pulled a notebook out of my bag. At some point during the night, I'd written down from memory what the lutin had said about John Berith as best I could:

- Seventh but not least
- Goes by many names. Sounds like different cultural mythologies
- Older than time
- Eats souls
- Travels with a child (because their energy is the purest)
- King of half-light?
- Walks unseen (invisible or because he looks normal?)

I read the list out loud to Gareth as we got onto the TransCanada Highway. "What do you think?" I asked. "Seventh but not least?"

"It makes sense when you put it next to that text from Carreau," he said. "Remember the poem— 'a devil that's human after all'? The poem describes seven devils, and the human one is the seventh. It also corresponds to what Carreau said about Berith appearing human. Maybe that's how he walks 'unseen'—because he can *imitate* by taking another form like a minion or *inhabit* another form like a malevolent. He's the 'King of half-light' because he can exist in the space between two planes but can enter and move around easily in either. And the fact that he's older than time explains why he has a lot of names. If he's some kind of malevolent super-being, then he could be cross-cultural instead of tied to one particular pantheon."

"And he always has a child with him so he can feed off their energy. For how long, I wonder. How many children through the years has he stolen? Julia, Nicky, Harmony, the little boy they talked about on the *Perchance To Dream* website—how many more before, after, and in between?"

"Not Julia," Gareth said tersely. "He killed her but he didn't keep her."

"I wonder why?" I asked.

"I doubt we'll ever know." Gareth gave a casual shrug but his hands gripped the steering wheel more tightly, a clear signal that it was too painful for him to discuss, at least when he was sober. "The more important question is how do we find him? And how the hell do we stop him?"

We were silent for a long time after that, each of us in our own head, trying to answer the questions that Gareth posed. Suddenly, my phone rang. I looked at the number— it was Horace so I put it on speaker phone.

"Verity, my dear!" Horace exclaimed. "How did it go in the delightful Saint-Cecile? Tell me everything now—I simply can't wait for your report."

I filled Horace in on the events at the Saint-Cecile church and he practically swooned. "Marvellous!" he decreed. "A 'lutin' you say? Intriguing. Of course, the true challenge will be finding enough genteel synonyms for excrement that my readers won't get too offended—or nauseated! Now, for the other reason why I've called you…" Horace paused expectantly.

"Tell me you've found out something about doppelgangers or disappearances involving look-alikes, anything strange like that," I prompted him.

"You're exactly right—I have indeed! I have a friend—a very dear friend named Quentin, a former police officer who happens to live in Thunder Bay. Or course, he *used* to live in Toronto, but retired up North because he couldn't stand the weather here. Out of the frying pan into the fire, I would say, but who am I to judge? I met him when I was a junior editor at a magazine called *Spectre*, many years ago, and he was investigating an…incident at our office. Funny story about that—the owner of *Spectre* was an exceptionally large woman named Sandy who was extremely fond of chihuahuas…"

I sat back in my seat and sighed. Horace had a habit of prolonging any conversation with one of his 'funny stories'. Gareth and I had learned a long time ago that listening to them would eventually get us around to whatever it was we really needed to know. It was a circuitous route but always worth it in the end. After a few minutes, Horace started to wind up, "…and the little terrors destroyed everything. Can you imagine?"

"Crazy," I responded, trying to sound engaged. "But Horace, what have you found out?"

"Oh, right!" he said. "Well, my friend Quentin now hosts a website in the same vein as '*Unsolved Mysteries*' and he did a little hunting through his archives. He found thirteen—yes, thirteen incidents of a child going missing under circumstances similar to your description where a look-alike or a double was involved, stretching back to the late 1800s. And those are only the recorded cases. If the internet had been invented during the Victorian period, I can hardly speculate how many more we might find! But as we *do* have the internet now, I'll be happy to send you the records that Quentin provided, as well as your fee from Father Paradis. Let me know if you need anything else. I'll start writing '*Le Diable de Saint-Cecile*' this very afternoon."

Horace rang off. I was impatient to see the records he would be sending, but that wouldn't be until much later — it was going to take more data than my phone could provide. We had booked into a campground just outside of Halifax in a place called Bedford, knowing that we'd be pulling in really late. As it was, we arrived a little before 9 pm. We got the trailer hooked up to the water system and Gareth took a shower while I got the wifi password and booted up our laptop. Sure enough, Horace had sent the files — there were over a dozen, some newspaper clippings, a few TV news reports, grainy photographs, and archived footage. It was a lot of terrible information to absorb: Curtis Hayes, age 7, taken from the beach; Mary Martin, age 6, went into the barn on a neighbour's farm and never came back out; Lorena DeSantos, age 8, disappeared during a church picnic...the list went on. The earliest case was Johannes Gingerich, who went missing in 1882. The article in the Halifax *Royal Gazette* stated that he had 'ventured too far from home'. In all the cases though, the children were last seen with someone they knew — a brother or sister, a parent, or in the case of Johannes, the local minister. And in each case, the person to last see them vehemently denied being present, especially the minister in Johannes's case who, despite his protests, was later hung for the crime. And in at least three of the cases, there was mention of a man, a regular, non-descript man who had been seen in the vicinity.

Gareth came out of the trailer, hair still slightly damp, and sat down across from me at the picnic table provided by the campsite. "I can tell by the look on your face that you've found something."

"Several somethings." I showed Gareth what Horace had sent. "I can't believe nobody put these together. All these cases have so much in common—why did no one see it?"

"They happened all over the country at different points in history. People didn't have national access to news until recently. They would have been looking for local patterns, not something countrywide. Even serial killers generally stay confined to a certain region—look at Clifford Olson or Paul Bernardo. And in all of the cases Horace sent you, the bodies were never found."

"Mary Martin disappeared in 1980…let's see here." I scanned the files. "The most recent case is from 1999. This one attracted national attention. Arjun Singh, 5 years old. Wandered away from his mother at the grocery store, never to be seen again. Security cameras in the parking lot showed him leaving with her, hanging onto the cart even, while his mother could clearly be seen on the store's internal cameras frantically looking for him. Authorities assumed he was taken by another woman who had deliberately disguised herself as his mother, and after a couple of months of futile searching, it became a cold case."

Gareth's brow furrowed. "I wonder…" he thought for a minute, reading through the files. "Mitchell's brother disappeared in the seventies, Mary Martin was taken in the eighties, Lorena DeSantos in 1990 and Arjun Singh in 1999. It's like there's a ten-year cycle—around ten years anyway. Maybe it depends on the age of the child. Arjun's cycle would have ended around the year 2009, we know that. What about the years in between him and Harmony then, between 2009 and 2014, like a missing link?"

"That makes sense, but I don't see anything in Horace's files. Maybe it was never reported. Maybe it was but Quentin overlooked it. I'll keep exploring."

"It's getting late," Gareth advised. "Go to bed. I'll call Mitchell, let him know we'll be over in the morning."

I protested mildly but I knew Gareth was right. Seeing all those faces, hearing all those heartbreaking stories was starting to wear on me, and I wanted to be sharp and focused for tomorrow and our meeting with Mitchell.

I got ready for bed. The campsite was humming with activity, but after a while, people started to put out their fires and settle in for the night. Eventually, all I could hear was crickets, and Gareth breathing steadily from the pull-out couch on the other side of the trailer. My eyes closed and I started to drift. Then suddenly, I was standing in the middle of an intersection in downtown Toronto near what looked like Dundas Square. There were hundreds of people waiting at the stoplights on each corner, and as the lights turned green, they all started walking, straight across and diagonally. I seemed to be rooted to the spot, and they were bumping into me, jostling me as if I wasn't there at all. I heard someone yelling and turned—in front of the Eaton Centre, a man was waving a pamphlet and shouting that the end of the world was coming. There was a little girl standing next to him, her curly black hair tied up with a pink bow. She was staring at the doomsayer, wide-eyed, but as I watched, I saw someone come up behind her. He was wearing a tan jacket and khaki pants, and he leaned down and whispered into her ear. She smiled and took the hand he offered her. They started to cross the street towards me, and as they got close, his eyes locked with mine, flashing that old familiar yellow. I was immobilized, feet glued to the asphalt, terrified. When he came up parallel to me, he stopped. His face was hard and his voice was a low, dangerous growl. "This is becoming tedious, hunter."

I tried to respond but my tongue was as paralyzed as my feet. Then the girl started tugging on his hand—he laughed and said, "Melody, don't be so impatient. The puppy is just across the street." He winked at me and transformed into a different man, one with the same curly black hair and dark skin as the little girl.

"Daddy, who are you talking to? Come *on*," the girl demanded, tugging harder on the hand she was clutching.

The man gave me a wide grin. "You're right, Melody. We shouldn't talk to strangers."

As they walked away, I screamed, "I know who you are!" and suddenly the faces of the people crossing the street around me changed until they were the faces of children, hundreds of children, all crying in a rising crescendo that drowned out my voice until the little girl and the monster who had stolen her disappeared. I gave one last scream, and then Gareth was shaking me awake.

"What is it? Tell me what you saw," he urged, as he tried to bring me out of the nightmare.

I finally opened my eyes and said, "I know who the missing link is."

14

MITCHELL'S STORY

I told Gareth about my nightmare, and we tried to look up missing children in the Toronto area from 2000 to 2014, but we got so many hits that it was a little overwhelming.

"He was disguised as a man—she called him 'Daddy'," I remembered. "And I'm pretty sure he called her 'Melody'. I don't see anything referencing that name, but there are so many cases—who knows?"

"It's going to be hard to narrow these down right now," Gareth agreed. We decided that we would wait until after we'd spoken to Mitchell and were back in Ontario to follow up. Gareth unhitched the truck from the fifth wheel—it was a complicated process involving blocking the wheels and unhooking cables and a variety of tricky manoeuvres, so we avoided it whenever we could, but neither of us wanted to drive into the North End of Halifax hauling it. Gareth finished up and tossed the duffel bag into the truck.

"Why are you taking that?" I asked.

"You never know," he said. "Better to be prepared. You and Mitchell have both been dreaming about John

Berith. What if putting the two of you in the same room creates a 'situation'?"

"Let's hope not! I'm nowhere near prepared for that. Not yet."

"Neither am I, really," Gareth admitted. "The most I could do is hold him off for a while. I'm pretty sure it's going to take something stronger than salt and vinegar to get rid of him. But I have a couple of ideas—I just need a little time. And maybe a chemistry lab."

I raised my eyebrows questioningly but Gareth wouldn't elaborate. "Better that you don't know in case you somehow dream about it," he said. "Gives me the element of surprise."

We drove into the North End of Halifax looking for the address that Mitchell had given us. It was a beautiful neighbourhood, with shops and parks lining the main street and the harbour in the distance. We found the side street where Mitchell lived and pulled up in front of a tiny bungalow. At first glance, it seemed well-kept, but as we got closer, I noticed that the flowerbeds were full of weeds and the paint around the windows was peeling. Gareth pulled his bag out of the truck. I raised an eyebrow. "Just in case," he reiterated.

We approached the front entrance, but before I had a chance to ring the bell, the door swung open. The man standing in the doorway was in his early sixties, with fine blonde hair and a wan, pale complexion, as if he hadn't been out in the sun for a while. Despite the warm weather, he was wearing a long-sleeved shirt. He smiled and said, "You must be Verity and Gareth. I'm Mitchell Cooper." He reached out his hand to shake mine, and the cuff of his shirt sleeve rode up, revealing a pattern of angry scars crisscrossing his wrist. I remembered what Horace had said, about him having a breakdown at the inquest and felt tremendous empathy for him. After Harmony's disappearance, I'd had moments myself where I'd felt like life wasn't worth living anymore. But we were both survivors, it seemed.

The interior of the bungalow was sparsely decorated in a haphazard way. Most of the furniture looked like it had come from second-hand stores. The most notable thing about the house was the sheer quantity of books. There were books stacked on the living room floor, books cramming the shelves, books on the kitchen table, books dog-eared or full of bookmarks identifying important pages. And the titles were all related to religion, philosophy, the supernatural, mysticism…it was obvious that Mitchell Cooper had spent the last few decades trying to understand what had happened to his brother.

"Excuse the mess," he said, grabbing a handful of books to make space on the couch for Gareth and me. "Please, make yourselves comfortable."

We all sat staring at each other for a minute. Finally, I broke the silence. "Uh, this is a nice neighbourhood. Have you lived here long?"

Mitchell sighed. "Actually, no. I moved here from Dartmouth about six months ago, right after my divorce."

"Oh, sorry." I felt terrible, and not comfortable at all, but Mitchell didn't seem to mind.

"I wasn't very good company. I don't blame her at all. She put up with this—" he waved his arm around at all the books, " — for years. It finally got to be too much. I really think I'm just better suited to being alone."

I could see Gareth nodding in a sympathetic way and I was a little taken aback. He was usually stoic to a fault. But it made sense; I'd never really considered why Gareth had never married—at least he'd never mentioned having a partner—but maybe he and Mitchell had more in common that I'd considered.

"We've come a long way," Gareth began. "Why don't you tell us about Nicholas."

That was all the prompting that Mitchell needed. He opened his mouth to speak and the words flooded out of him.

Mitchell Cooper was five years old when his brother Nicholas was born. They were close growing up out of necessity. Their father was a hard man, an alcoholic prone to fits of violence, and Mitch quickly became the protector, putting himself in harm's way to stop his father from taking out his anger on little Nicky. Their mother was a timid woman, herself pummeled into submission by her overbearing and physically abusive husband. There were more days than Mitch could count where he was forced to stay home from school until the bruises healed.

"The teachers all thought I had some terrible illness," he said, "and my mother kept up that illusion for years to shield my father from blame."

The day Nicky disappeared was triggered by a particularly awful set of circumstances. Their mother had gotten a flat tire coming home from the grocery store the previous afternoon, so not only was their father outraged over the expense of having to call a tow truck, but the dinner wasn't ready on time as well, and that had sent him into a drunken frenzy the likes of which neither of them had seen. Their mother had locked herself in the bathroom after a terrible beating, and their father had spent an hour alternating between tossing back shots of rye whiskey and screaming and slamming his fists against the bathroom door to no avail before he turned his attention and frustration to the boys, taking his belt to each of them in turn until bedtime. The violence continued into the next day when he finally passed out. Their mother, taking advantage, fled the house to her sister's, leaving the boys alone to bear the brunt of it when he woke up. Terrified, Mitch ran to his room, grabbed the two dollars his mother had given him the week before when he'd turned unlucky thirteen, and whispered to Nicky, "Let's go." They went out through Mitch's bedroom window and took off to the park.

It was a hot afternoon, one of the last days in August before school started again, and the park was full of kids all trying to cram the most out of the summer before returning to the confines of the classroom. When Mitch and his little brother arrived, they headed straight to the playground, full of all kinds of swings, slides, and climbing equipment. Nicky was young enough that his enthusiasm soon made him forget about the trouble at home. Mitch was old enough to understand that escape was only temporary, but still, he was able to derive some enjoyment out of seeing Nicky so carefree, at least for a few moments.

After an hour of hard play, Nicky ran up to him breathless. "Can we get some ice cream? Please?" He pointed at the concession stand across from the baseball diamonds.

Mitch, knowing their time was becoming increasingly limited, and that the reality of going home would soon overshadow his and Nicky's reprieve, said, "I'll get it. You stay here and keep playing. But don't leave, okay? Wait for me to come back. You want Tiger Stripe?"

Nicky nodded enthusiastically and sprinted back to the climbing equipment. Mitch made his way over to the concession stand, looking over his shoulder every once in a while to ensure that he could still see his brother's green t-shirt. There was a line-up, and while he waited, he struck up a conversation with the girl behind him. He was thirteen and starting to develop an interest in the opposite sex; she was pretty and chatty. He got up to the counter and ordered—Tiger Stripe for Nicky and Mint Chocolate Chip for himself, which still left a little change in his pocket from the five dollars he'd started with—then headed back to the playground, not even realizing that he hadn't watched for the green of his little brother's t-shirt in at least ten minutes. Still, Nicky had promised not to wander, hadn't he? And he was old enough to know better, wasn't he? But when Mitch arrived at the edge of the playground, ice cream starting to drip down his hands in the heat, he couldn't see Nicky anywhere. He was angry at first—hadn't he told Nicky to stay put? But the anger soon turned to trepidation as he walked the perimeter, no Nicky to be seen anywhere. He didn't know what to do. He searched for an hour, finally throwing the ice cream cones in the garbage, too melted to eat, and railed internally at his brother. The birthday money was wasted, and the realization that by now their father would have woken up and noticed they'd snuck out, and would be waiting with the belt (or worse) made him half-furious and half-petrified. Finally, out of options, he found a woman sitting on a park bench watching her own children playing on the slide.

"Excuse me," he began timidly, unused to adults, too used to their unpredictability. "I've lost my brother. He was supposed to wait for me here but he's gone."

The woman smiled. "Are you sure he didn't go home?"

Mitch shook his head. "He wouldn't. Not without me."

"Where are your parents?"

Mitch hesitated. The woman, taking in the welts on his arms and the slight bruising around one eye, nodded. "There's a park attendant over by the grandstand next to the woods. Let's go talk to him."

And that was when the nightmare truly began. The park attendant was surprised. "But I saw you and a younger boy run past me into the forest about an hour ago. Then you came out not long after."

Mitch protested. He'd been at the concession stand, then at the playground searching; he hadn't gone near the woods. There was a girl who could prove it. But the girl was gone, and the park attendant was adamant. "It was you. Right down to that Dodgers jersey."

And that was when Mitch knew that his life would be forever changed. The police were called, and a search started. His parents were brought to the park: his mother, trembling and covered in bruises, his father boozy and red-faced with barely restrained fury at being torn away from beer and football, not even aware that the two boys were gone.

"What did you do, you little piece of dogdirt?" his father hissed at him. Mitch shook his head, knowing that no matter what, he would most likely be dead by morning. The thrashing inflicted upon him at home later was so severe that his mother finally found the courage to call for help.

Mitch was taken into protective custody and never saw either of his parents again until over 6 years later, at the inquest into Nicky's disappearance. He was nineteen by then, out of foster care and on his own, working the night desk at a shady motel in Digby when he was called to testify. He'd been cleared by the police years before—the parents of the girl he'd spoken to in line had brought her forward. She'd confirmed that he was nowhere near the woods at the time the park attendant claimed to have seen him, and the ice cream vendor who had served him Tiger Stripe and Mint Chocolate Chip agreed with her. Still, a cloud of suspicion hung over him no matter where he went, to the point that he even doubted himself. Had it been him? Had he somehow managed to split himself in two? Was there a part of him that was evil, that was sick of deflecting the violence away from Nicky onto himself? Was it possible that he could have hurt his little brother, even killed him?

He was plagued by questions and nightmares, and sunk into a deep depression, made worse by seeing his parents staring at him as he took the witness stand. His father was hostile; his mother was blank, as if she had no idea who he was, and that was worse. When he was asked to recall the events leading up to his brother's disappearance, he broke down sobbing, and started to scream incoherently about the creature in his dreams that looked just like him and had stolen his brother.

"It was a few days later when I did this," he said quietly to Gareth and me, pulling up his sleeves to fully reveal the scars I'd glimpsed earlier. "Luckily, when I didn't show up for my shift at work, the manager came knocking on my door. When I didn't answer, he broke the door down and found me. I was close to gone, but they brought me back. Some days I'm not sure if that was a good thing or not."

"It was." I put my hand on his arm. "Because now we all know we're not crazy. John Berith is real, and the damage he's done is real too. But together, we can stop him from doing this to anyone else."

"I'll help you in whatever way you need me to."

Gareth leaned forward, his elbows on his knees, his hands clasped together. "Good. Now here's what we know about John Berith. Have you ever heard of something called a 'malevolent'?"

Mitchell shook his head, and Gareth began to talk.

15

HALIFAX PART TWO

When Gareth was finished, Mitchell sagged back into his chair, eyes closed, and exhaled in what seemed like relief. We waited silently, not sure whether or not he was going to believe us, or laugh hysterically at us. Finally, he opened his eyes.

"For years, I doubted myself," he said, waving his arm at the piles of books that took up all the available space in the room. "I thought, 'Surely this is a waste of time. No wonder you're alone. No wonder Pascale left you. What woman would want to live like this, with an obsessed fool like you?' But now, you're telling me none of this was in vain? Thank you." He closed his eyes again.

"Thank *you*," I replied. "If it wasn't for you and your dreams, we wouldn't be as close to stopping John Berith as we are."

"But how exactly do we do that?" Mitchell leaned forward, looking perplexed. "I mean, I understand that these… malevolent creatures inhabit people's bodies, but if John Berith has been stealing children for hundreds of years, whose body is he in? Wouldn't the man be dead by now, or is a malevolent capable of making someone immortal?"

"We think he's been inhabiting a series of bodies. As one gets too old, he chooses another. Every account describes the man the same way: ordinary, regular, like anyone else. Berith must look for a specific type. Gareth and I once encountered a minor malevolent inhabiting a cat—don't laugh," I said, suppressing a smile myself as Mitchell's eyebrows shot up and the corner of his mouth twitched. "I know it sounds funny but it was pretty intimidating. Anyway, once we'd gotten rid of the malevolent, the cat seemed back to its old self, perfectly normal."

"As normal as a cat can be," muttered Gareth under his breath. I rolled my eyes and ignored him.

"Aside from being a little sleepy, it seemed fine. So maybe it's the same approximate ten-year cycle as the children—Berith inhabits someone until he's got what he needs, then the person is left back where they started, just a little confused or disoriented."

"How could they live for even a day with a malevolent inside them? Wouldn't they remember everything he made them do? How could they not remember the children?"

"Hypothetically," Gareth stated, "the creature would find a man to inhabit in order to stalk the child it wanted, then steal her …or him. The man would dispose of the child to give the malevolent the energy it required and eventually, the malevolent would dispose of the man. To whoever was inhabited, it would probably seem like a terrible nightmare, nothing more."

"So an ordinary man would be used to kill a child, just so this John Berith could steal the child's energy?" Mitchell was appalled. "It would make any man insane!"

"We don't know they're dead!" I interjected.

"Verity, we've talked about this…" Gareth said gently.

"We don't know. Not for sure," I insisted. Logically, rationally, I knew that Harmony was gone, but my heart hung on to the possibility that somehow, she could be brought back. It made no sense, but if an evil spirit could inhabit a man and feed off human energy, then wasn't anything possible?

Nobody said anything for a minute, then Mitchell had a sudden thought. "What about the doppelgangers? If Berith uses a real person to steal these children, then why disguise itself as me, or Verity, or someone's mother or father?"

"Easier to lure them that way," Gareth answered. "Nicky was seven years old—would he have gone off with a stranger? Arjun was in a grocery store, and most likely would have started screaming, or doing something to attract attention if a man he didn't know tried to take him."

"And Harmony knew that if anything happened, she was supposed to go straight home. She was too smart to leave the bus stop with a stranger, no matter what he promised her," I said emphatically, remembering Melody and what the man had said to her about a puppy.

"So John Berith is a malevolent that can not only inhabit someone, but can enter our dreams." Mitchell shook his head in disbelief. "If he can shape shift as well, who knows what else he's capable of?"

"I suppose we'll find out," Gareth said flatly. "It's time we deal with this malevolent, once and for all."

"What's the plan? What's our next step?" Mitchell asked.

"*Our* next step?" I echoed. "I'm not sure—Gareth and I have to go back to Ontario...."

Mitchell was adamant. "Then I'm coming too. If John Berith is as powerful as we think, you're going to need all the help you can get. I have a stake in this and you're not doing it without me. There's nothing in this world that will give me more satisfaction than helping to send this...thing back to whatever hell it came from."

"Oh, we're not sending it anywhere," Gareth said. "The goal is to destroy it. But first, we need to find it."

After some debate, we all agreed that there was no point in Mitchell coming back with us right away. "OK. I can be in Toronto in under three hours," he said. "Call me when you need me and I'll be on the next flight."

He made us all a late lunch, and then offered to investigate our missing link. "I've become a pretty thorough researcher over the years. I've got subscriptions to hundreds of newspapers *and* their archives. If there's any information about the girl you dreamed about, Melody, I'll find it. Think back—is there anything from the dream that might give us a better sense of the year she was taken?"

I closed my eyes, trying to call up the images from my dream. The room was silent as I concentrated. Dundas Square, the Eaton Centre, storefronts along the street, a billboard—what was on the billboard? I focused harder and the billboard became more clear. "It's an ad for a movie. A huge blue face, kind of alien-looking…that's all I can see."

"Hmmm," Mitchell pondered for a moment. "Sounds like that James Cameron film *Avatar*, maybe." He went over to a desk in the corner and pushed aside some books to reveal a laptop. "Just a sec." After a minute, he turned the laptop to face us. "Look familiar?" he asked.

I stared at the image on his screen. "That's it," I confirmed. "No question."

"Okay," Mitchell smiled. "Our first clue. *Avatar* came out in 2009. I'll start there."

Gareth and I left Mitchell at his computer, with the promise that we would contact him as soon as we got back to Ontario and had a plan in place.

"And if I find out anything about our missing link, I'll let you know right away," he assured us.

We were walking down the driveway towards the truck when Gareth suddenly turned on me. "You shouldn't have done that," he said harshly, his face stormy.

I was confused. "Done what?"

"You can't hold out false hope like that. Look what he's gone through, what he's done to himself out of guilt. Those children—they're all dead! There's no changing that fact—the only thing we can do is find them and lay them to rest. Think whatever else you want, as impossible as it may be, but keep it to yourself from now on." He walked away from me and my jaw dropped. In the almost two years we'd been together, Gareth had *never* spoken to me that way. He might as well have slapped me in the face. I was stunned and the tears came unbidden to my eyes. I held my breath and tried to stop the wrenching sob that was threatening to escape my lungs, but I couldn't. Gareth heard.

"Verity, I—" But I didn't hear the rest. I took off running down the street blindly, no destination in mind. I just needed to escape from all of the horror, from the guilt, the despair, and the undeniable truth that Harmony was gone, that there was no bringing her back, and that I would never hold her hand again or hear her call me Veevee. I'd been fooling myself this whole time that there was magic in the world but there wasn't. There was only evil.

The harbour was in the distance, the water glinting in the sunlight. I slowed to a walk. I found the entrance to a park and I made my way to a bench where I could sit and clear my head for a minute. The afternoon sun was warm and there were birds singing in the trees that lined the park. It could have been an idyllic moment, but I was wracked with worry. What if Gareth just left me here? What if he was so furious that he decided not to wait for me? I was trying to formulate a plan, figure out some way to get back to Ontario, get my car from Horace, and kill John Berith on my own, when I heard someone coming, breathing raggedly. I twisted my neck to glance behind me, expecting a jogger but hoping for something else. My heart leapt. It was Gareth, winded and upset. I turned away again, trying not to look relieved. He sat down heavily next to me and dropped his duffel bag at his feet.

"You run fast," he said, leaning back to catch his breath.

"Keep up, old man," I said matter-of-factly, disguising my elation at his appearance.

"Well, I had the additional burden of this bag. It's heavy."

"We all have our burdens," I answered quietly.

"I need to remember that, be a little more considerate. Maybe start exercising more too."

I laughed. "That goes for both of us. I'm exhausted." I was about to reassure him that I understood what he meant, and that I was giving up the fantasy that Harmony could possibly be alive, when I realized that a group of people was slowly approaching us. "Who are *they*?"

Gareth squinted in the direction I was pointing. "I don't see anyone…wait—there are a *lot* of shimmers…and more coming." There was another group of people further away, coming from the other side of the park, dressed in what looked like costumes from the early 1900s. The first group was getting closer. There was a woman in the lead, her expression mournful. In the distance behind them, more people were gathering in what seemed to be a mob of men, women, and children. "The Halifax harbour explosion," Gareth whispered to me. "Two ships collided in the harbour and one of them was full of munitions for the war. The blast leveled this whole area, killed almost two thousand people."

"What do they want?" I whispered back, feeling slightly afraid at the sheer number of spirits getting closer to us by the second.

"I didn't have time to lock my bag in the truck—I didn't want to lose sight of you," Gareth said. "It's the box. They must be able to sense it."

The woman in the lead was in front of us now. Her face was filthy and her clothes were covered in blood. Her mouth opened and her voice was raw with desperation.

"Please," she begged, extending her hand towards us. "Please. It's been so long."

There was a young man behind her, no older than me, dressed in a naval uniform. "Help me," he implored. "I want my mother. Please, I want to see my mother again."

"Why are there so many?!" I exclaimed to Gareth, panic rising in my chest. "Why didn't they cross over on their own?"

"From my knowledge of history, the explosion happened so suddenly that they would have had no idea what hit them," Gareth said quickly and quietly. "Everything within a half mile was leveled and more than a thousand people were killed instantly. They're confused, probably didn't even realize they were dead at first."

As Gareth spoke, he leaned down to open the duffel bag and pulled out the box. At the sight of it, the cries from the mob amplified. Children started wailing and the woman in front of us began sobbing with gratitude. "Salvation! Finally!" Ghostly tears ran down her grimy face and she gestured to the crowd. "He's here! He is the one!" She reached out her hand. Gareth had no choice but to open the lid. She vanished with a euphoric sigh. At the sound, the crowd began to press forward from all sides, their arms reaching out to us in supplication. Gareth looked around wildly as the shimmers descended on him. As he stood there, box open, concentrating on crossing as many of the crowd over as he could—young, old, men, women, boys, and girls—I could see the effort was taking its toll on him and he was starting to flag, getting weaker with every shimmer that was sucked into the box.

Finally, he fell to his knees and I knew he couldn't take much more—he was on the verge of complete collapse—and I yelled, "Enough! Only the children and then he has to stop! But I promise we'll come back!"

The crowd gave a collective gasp. "No!" a man beseeched. "Let us go! Help us!" The crowd roared in agreement.

"He can't!" I shouted back at the crowd. "It will kill him and then *none* of you will be free!" There was a pause, and then a commotion as over a dozen children were led up to the front of the crowd.

One little girl, about five years old, looked at me wide-eyed and asked, "Are you my mother?"

I thought my heart would break, but I answered with a confident smile, "No, but you'll see her very soon. Be brave and give me your hand." She did, and I guided it towards Gareth.

As she began to disappear, her face lit up in recognition. "Mama!" she cried, and then she was gone. I helped the other children one at a time until there were none left.

"It's done," I whispered to Gareth, who sank to the ground, exhausted. Then I turned back to the crowd.

"We'll return. I give you my word." I took Gareth by the arm and helped him pull himself up onto the park bench. He shoved the box inside the duffel bag and the crowd sighed, a long suspiration that tailed off into the wind. As it did, they began to vanish until there was no one left.

"Are you all right?" I put my hand on his shoulder. "Do you want to stay here while I get the truck?"

"No," he laughed sardonically. "But maybe we can make our way back more slowly than we arrived."

As we walked away, I could have sworn I heard a forlorn voice carried by the wind. "Don't forget…," it whispered.

"Don't worry," I answered softly. "We won't."

16

THE STOLEN CHILD

The journey back to Ontario was worrisome, despite it being uneventful. We had spent our last night at the campground recovering from the impromptu mass crossover, and by the time Gareth had hooked the fifth wheel back up to the truck, he was completely done in. Even though we knew we shouldn't, Gareth opened the pullout couch in the trailer and fell into a deep sleep while I drove the first leg, hoping we wouldn't get pulled over. The first leg turned into the second leg, and when it started to get dark, I found a parking lot to stretch out in and get some rest. In the morning, I tried to shake him awake but he muttered, "Just a couple more hours," then fell back unconscious again.

When we crossed the Quebec/Ontario border on the 401, I was still behind the wheel. I was incredibly concerned about Gareth—I had no idea that helping spirits transition affected him so much. We'd only ever done one at a time prior to Halifax; seeing him with his energy so drained was frightening and I was glad I'd been there to stem the rising tide of the dead. And what did the woman mean, "He is the one"? She made him seem like a saviour, which I supposed to a certain extent he was, at least for the spirits left behind after the Halifax explosion. Thinking back, I realized that I'd never actually used the box myself; Gareth was always the one to hold it, and maybe there was good reason why. But what that reason might be, I wasn't certain.

Finally, my phone rang, a signal from Gareth that he was awake and ready to take over the wheel. I pulled onto the shoulder, got out, and met him at the door.

"Are you sure?" The last thing I wanted was for him to start driving and then get weak again once we hit heavy traffic—at least the roads were really quiet right now.

He waved me off. "I'll be fine. Call Horace and see if he has anything for us."

Horace was delighted as always to hear from me. "I hope my files were of some assistance?"

"It was a lot to get through but extremely helpful," I assured him. "Tell Quentin we're very grateful."

"I will..." Horace paused. "But you *are* going to tell me why you needed them, aren't you? What are you and dear Gareth up to, chasing doppelgangers? I'm dying to know what your little side project is all about, especially since you've gone all the way to Halifax for it."

"Oh, that's a long story, Horace—"

"Well then, I have the perfect plan," he interrupted. "Why don't you swing by here now that you're back in Ontario? I'll invite Quentin, and we can dine al fresco on the terrace while you fill us in."

"I don't know, Horace," I demurred. "We're pretty road-weary right now." I wasn't sure how much we wanted to tell Horace at this point—we weren't even certain ourselves what the next step might be, but Horace was insistent.

"Nonsense! It's not that much further, and as an added incentive, you can park that rickety rig behind the house and spend the night. I have several guest bedrooms in this old place—wouldn't you love a real mattress and a proper shower for a change?"

I had to admit I was sorely tempted. "All right," I said. "I'll talk to Gareth. I'm not promising anything though."

Gareth considered Horace's proposal silently for a few minutes. I could tell he was weighing the pros and cons. Finally, he said, "I suppose we'll have to tell him eventually. It might be good to get his input—as well as Quentin's. And a comfortable bed would be nice for a change. The pullout is getting pretty lumpy."

"I thought you loved that old couch," I protested. "If you want to swap and take the bunk, I don't mind. I keep forgetting that you're so much older than me. Is it rheumatism or the gout that people get at your age?" I teased, trying to keep a straight face.

Gareth snorted. "Watch it, missy. Your time will come."

I laughed and called Horace back. He was elated. "I'll let Quentin know right now! Luckily, he's here for a visit. Ooh—do you and dear Gareth prefer chicken or salmon...maybe I should do coq au vin...or salmon wellington..."

His enthusiasm was contagious and I found myself actually excited about the prospect of a dinner with normal human people, and a soft bed to curl up in. I told him we were fine with whatever menu he decided on—after days of driving, and eating at fast food restaurants or roadside stands, we were simply happy to have something other than soggy burgers.

An hour went by. Gareth was listening to some call-in show on CBC and I was trying to doze when the phone rang. It was Mitchell—he sounded excited.

"I think I found your missing link," he said. "I went through the Toronto Star archives and found mention of a young girl, Melody Benoit. Apparently, she went missing in July 2009. She was 7 years old at the time."

"Why wouldn't Quentin have had any information about her?" I wondered.

"It was a tricky case. The police had a hard time believing the mother—she and the father were in a custody battle and Melody was last seen with a man matching the father's description. They assumed he had taken the girl out of the country, even though they were never able to find either of them. But get this—the mom considered herself a bit of a psychic, said she'd had dreams about a man with a beige car, a cabin near a large body of water, and hundreds of bones. The police dismissed her as seeking attention—"

"Wait! Did you say beige?" I felt a chill come over me. I'd spent hours and hours obsessing over security camera footage of a beige car parked near where Harmony was last seen, hoping that I might find some clue, no matter how small, to her disappearance. "I need to talk to her. Where is she?"

Mitchell's tone became sombre. "Unfortunately, she passed away a few years ago. Cancer. Does the car mean something to you?"

I sighed, gravely disappointed. "Yes, maybe. There was a beige car seen where my sister disappeared, but no one ever came forward and it was never found. It's a shame the police wouldn't listen to Melody's mother. If only they had, Harmony might not be…gone." Even though I'd made my peace with Gareth and accepted the truth, I couldn't yet bring myself to say the word 'dead' out loud. "It doesn't matter," I said. "It's still my fault. I should have been there at the bus stop that day."

Mitchell was silent for a moment. "And if I hadn't gone for ice cream…" his voice choked.

"Don't say that!" I admonished him. "You can't blame yourself. You were just a kid."

"So were you. Don't ever forget that. But you're right. The only person—or thing—to blame is John Berith, wherever he may be."

Mitchell and I said our goodbyes and I promised him we'd be in touch as soon as we needed him to come. Hopefully, that would be sooner than later.

We pulled into Horace's driveway about four in the afternoon. He came out to greet us and directed Gareth as we backed down the laneway to the large garage behind the house. Horace was an amazing sight, dressed in a snowy white tuxedo, complete with a deep purple cummerbund and bowtie. My heart sank.

"I didn't realize it was a fancy dinner," I said glumly. "I don't have anything nice to wear. There's not much call for high fashion in our business."

Horace laughed lightly as he guided us through the back door into his house. "This old thing? I've had it forever! Never fear, Verity my love. Wear whatever you like—it's the quality of the company that counts, not the designer on the label. And you and Gareth are always the best company."

His kindness continued as he showed us upstairs to our rooms. They were luxurious, something out of a magazine, and each with its own bathroom. Mine, decorated in tones of lavender with vintage paintings of Paris lining the walls, had an ensuite complete with a soaker tub. When he saw my eyes go wide, he whispered, "There's time before dinner for a nice hot bath if you like." I took his advice. After grabbing some clothes from the trailer—my best jeans and cleanest t-shirt—I ran the bath and settled into the warm water. But I found myself unable to truly enjoy it; without anything to focus on, my mind started racing and I couldn't relax. Finally, I pulled the plug, literally and figuratively, on the bathtub and got dressed for dinner. As I came downstairs, I could hear voices coming from Horace's large parlour. Gareth was already there, tidied up and looking better than he had in the last two days. Horace, resplendent in his tuxedo, was talking in an animated way to Gareth and another man who I assumed must be Quentin. He was handsome, and although he must have been around the same age as Horace, he had a young-looking face. I was happy to see that he was wearing a simple button-down shirt and linen pants. When he saw me, he seemed relieved as well.

"I thought I was seriously underdressed for the occasion," he said, holding out his hand and taking mine. "Trust Horace to appear like the belle of the ball and put us all to shame. I'm Quentin."

"Verity Darkwood," I replied over Horace's protests.

Quentin put his arm affectionately around Horace's shoulders. "I'm only teasing. You look wonderful as always, although how you keep that white suit in such pristine condition will never cease to amaze me."

We all laughed, and I was surprised at how comfortable I felt. I'd always been an introvert and I wasn't used to being in groups of people, especially over the last couple of years when it had just been Gareth and me. But Quentin had a sense of calm around him that appealed to me, and Horace—well, it was hard to feel awkward around Horace, who was the consummate host.

After introductions and a few minutes of small talk, Horace served us all drinks, then led us to the terrace. "I'll be right back," he called over his shoulder as he disappeared down the hall. We sat down, and in no time, Horace was back, wheeling a trolley laden with plates. He'd chosen to go with salmon and the meal was spectacular, better than anything I'd ever eaten, When I expressed my gratitude, Horace was pleased.

"It's nothing, my dear," he said modestly, wiping his mouth delicately with a cloth napkin.

"He's been in the kitchen all afternoon," Quentin whispered to me. "But he loves it!"

Finally, the meal was over and at Horace's insistence, we "retired" to the parlour. We'd barely gotten comfortable when he began peppering us with questions. "I've been filling Quentin in on your adventures. Now what's going on? You *must* tell us!"

Gareth hesitated and looked at me. I gave him a silent go-ahead, and he spoke. "We're looking for a super-malevolent who's been kidnapping children for at least a hundred years but most likely for much longer. It uses the children's energy to sustain itself, then disposes of them once they're drained. It calls itself John Berith — at least it does here. It inhabits the bodies of ordinary men, and can disguise itself as other people. Based on the information you provided to us, we know it had a cycle of about ten years before it needed to be replenished, but that cycle seems to be getting shorter. We need to destroy it before it can take another child."

There was a long silence. Horace and Quentin seemed lost for words. I continued, "We know that the most recent unsolved child abductions reported have been Lorena DeSantos in 1990, Arjun Singh in 1999, and Melody Benoit in 2009, all under similar circumstance as my sister, who was taken in 2014, only 5 years later than Melody for some reason. But if the cycle really *is* getting shorter, we know he's due within the next couple of years and we already have evidence that he's been prowling around." I didn't mention anything about Julia or Mitchell's brother Nicky — best to keep it simple for now. I sat back and waited for one of them to speak.

Finally, Horace said, "I'm deeply sorry about your sister. I knew, of course, about Harmony, as well as Gareth's Julia." Gareth looked at him sharply but Horace waved his hand lightly. "I'd vetted you thoroughly before making the offer to become business associates, but there never seemed to be the right time to mention it."

"Then you know why we're so motivated to resolve this," I said.

Horace nodded. "There are dozens of names in those files Quentin put together. So many children."

"Yes," Gareth agreed. "Too many." He paused then continued gruffly, "I don't think we can include Julia in the cycle. She was...," his voice broke slightly, "killed by Berith but it didn't keep her." He said nothing else but I knew how difficult it was for him to even mention it.

Quentin seemed lost in thought for a moment, then turned to me. "Did you say Melody Benoit? Clarice Benoit's daughter?"

"I did. Do you know the case?" I asked.

"I didn't realize it *was* a case, but yes, I'm familiar with it. So she was right, after all? Poor woman." We all looked at him expectantly and he continued. "Clarice Benoit was a rather well-known writer and an amateur spiritualist. She published several novels, mostly thrillers, but before she died in 2014, she put out a poetry collection that won a couple of prestigious awards. She dedicated the collection to Melody, and most of the pieces in the collection are about her daughter's disappearance—some of it is really heart-wrenching. I read an interview with her once where she talked about her visions, particularly one in which she saw her daughter's bones rising out of a swamp. It was haunting. She knew she was dying at that point, told the interviewer that she would carry her fury into the next life and lay waste to heaven until she got her daughter back."

"Maybe that's exactly what she did," Gareth offered. "You said Clarice passed away in 2014—that was when Berith took Harmony. Might account for the shortened cycle."

Horace stood up abruptly and left the room. We could hear him rummaging around upstairs. After a few minutes, he reappeared, a book in his hand. "I have a copy of her poetry collection here." The title on the worn cover was *What Remains*. He opened it to a dog-eared page. "This piece is called *The Stolen Child*." He began to read in a solemn voice.

> *You were ripped away from me*
> *And then returned,*
> *An empty frame.*
> *I held you, gripped your edges*
> *To reform you*
> *Love transcending horror*
> *Anger transcending grief.*

I would burn the world
To hear your voice again
Your whisper in my ear
Your breath against my neck
Your hand in my hand
The bones white and cold and small
And never letting go.

When Horace was finished reading, he shut the book and closed his eyes. Quentin said quietly, "Very powerful."

Horace looked at us tearfully and sniffed. "They're all like this one—full of grief and desolation. A mother who's lost a child is a force to be reckoned with. I know my own mother never got over it." He clutched the book tight against his chest. "One of my earliest memories is toddling out to the tree in the yard of the house where I grew up. There was a girl there, sitting on a tire swing. My older sister Miranda, but I called her Mimi." He smiled nostalgically. "She was my best friend. We spent hours out there, talking and laughing every day. I think I must have been around 7 years old when it occurred to me that I was growing up, but Mimi hadn't changed at all. I realized that none of the pictures in the house of her were taken after her sixth birthday, and then I knew why I wasn't allowed to talk about her, why my mother got so upset when I mentioned her. Mimi had died, you see. She'd fallen out of that tree and broken her poor little neck three years before I was born. It was with a child's simplicity that I accepted that Mimi lived under the tree and never got older. But my mother—she could never accept any of it. The day after I left home for university, she had the tree cut down, and I never saw my sister again. My mother's grief for Mimi overshadowed my entire childhood. I never forgave her for cutting down the tree, but I understood why she did it."

Quentin leaned forward and patted Horace's hand. Horace smiled wanly. "Whatever you need from us, we'll be happy to provide it."

Horace placed the book reverently on the coffee table next to him, face down, the photograph of Clarice Benoit staring up at us. Suddenly, Gareth blanched and gasped.

"Is that Clarice Benoit?" He seemed astounded.

"Yes," Horace answered. "Taken not long before she passed away. Why?"

Gareth shook his head in disbelief. "Two years ago, I was in Cochrane, working the mines. One night I had a dream. In it, the woman on the back cover of that book, Clarice Benoit, although I didn't know it at the time, appeared to me. She told me to pack up, drive south to Kincardine. She said I would meet my truth there, and that would help me find peace. I had nothing to lose so I did as she said."

"And you met your truth," Horace smiled. "You met Verity."

"Maybe by peace, she meant Harmony," I added. "Even in the next life, Clarice Benoit is a force to be reckoned with."

Quentin nodded in agreement. We all said goodnight then, none of us really up for any more conversation after Gareth's revelation. Gareth and I planned to leave in the morning and head to Windsor, where there was a family whose house was being haunted by a parrot. "It should be a simple one," said Horace, "but it will make a wonderful story for *The Echo*. Apparently, the bird swears like a sailor!"

I got ready for bed, then sank into the luxury of the thick mattress Horace had promised me. He was right; it was definitely better than that thin piece of foam that I slept on in the trailer. I snuggled under the duvet, but I couldn't sleep. I kept thinking about Gareth's revelation from earlier, and that it wasn't fate that had brought us together after all, that Clarice Benoit was somehow able to engineer it from beyond the grave. I remembered those lines from the poem Horace had read: "*Your hand in my hand, The bones white and cold and small, And never letting go.*" I knew exactly how Clarice felt, that longing to hold a beloved child's little hand one last time, even if it *was* just bones. Eventually, I couldn't resist the comfort of the bed and I drifted off.

I was awake with the sun and was getting packed up when there was a knock on my door. It was Gareth. "Horace got an email late last night that he wants to tell us about."

We headed downstairs, the smell of bacon and eggs beckoning us towards the kitchen. We found Horace standing by the stove, wearing an apron. "There you are!" he exclaimed. "You'll find this very interesting. Do you remember Tanis Gibson? You rid her of a pesky phantom if I remember correctly. Well, she emailed last night, a terribly angry missive full of accusations. Apparently, we're all charlatans!"

"Why?" I asked. "What happened?"

"It seems," Horace replied, "that Poltergeist Pat is back."

17

THE RETURN OF POLTERGEIST PAT

"What?" I exclaimed.

"I know," Horace replied, wiping his hands on his apron fretfully. "Of all the nerve. I believe her actual term was 'rip-off artists'."

I turned to Gareth. "Uncle Pat is back?"

"Not a good sign." Then he got a curious look on his face. "Or maybe it is."

Horace's eyes widened with consternation. "What on earth are you two talking about? This sounds very mysterious! Is there something you neglected to tell me about this particular assignment?"

"Well," I began sheepishly, "we didn't exactly cross the poltergeist over. He wasn't trying to cause any problems—he was wreaking havoc at the house in Washington to warn the family about John Berith. It seemed like the super-malevolent might have had its sights set on Tanis's daughter but the poltergeist—Uncle Pat—somehow put it on notice that it wasn't welcome. We left Pat there with the promise that he'd find a way to let us know if Berith was back."

"And if Pat's acting up again, it looks like Berith is," added Gareth. "Do you have a number for Tanis? We should contact her, arrange a visit right away. Sorry, but the parrot will have to wait."

"Let me speak to her," Horace offered. "She seemed quite upset. Don't worry—I can be extremely persuasive when I need to be."

I laughed. "We're aware, Horace. Please don't take 'no' for an answer. We *need* to talk to Uncle Pat. It could be the only way we can locate John Berith, or at least whoever the super-malevolent is inhabiting right now."

Gareth and I waited while Horace made the call. We were trying not to eavesdrop, but it was difficult to avoid. From what we could tell from Horace's side of the conversation, it was a hard sell. "I've worked with them for years... very honest...I assure you...more than one type of spirit, you see...very old house...Better Business Bureau?!...free of charge for the second cleansing...absolutely... a full refund? I'd have to consider...all right then. I'll let them know."

He hung up and came back into the kitchen, sweating slightly. "The woman drives a hard bargain. She's agreed, however, to entertain a second visit under certain financial conditions that you need not worry about—"

"We don't want to be paid," I interrupted. "This is more important than money. When is she expecting us?"

"As soon as possible, she said. Our misbehaving miscreant has gone from throwing things out of the medicine cabinet to writing warnings on the mirror—using her *favourite* lipstick, she insisted on telling me."

"We can make it by lunch if we leave soon," Gareth said. "Pack up, Verity. There's no time to waste if Berith is there for the reason we think it is. Call Mitchell too. He'll want to come as soon as possible."

Mitchell, true to his word, was ready to leave at a moment's notice after I explained what was going on. "I can fly out at 8:55 Halifax time and arrive in London around noon your time," he said calmly, as if I was asking him to attend a business meeting. "I'll arrange a rental car and meet you at the house a little after 1 pm. Text me the address."

We left Horace's after eating breakfast hastily. The food was delicious, but I hardly tasted it, I was so anxious. As we were finishing, Horace was putting together a tray. "For Quentin," he smiled with a twinkle in his eye.

I hugged Horace goodbye. "Be careful, my lovely," he said. "I'd be devastated if anything happened to you or dear Gareth."

We got in the truck and Gareth said, "I didn't realize that Horace and Quentin…"

"Really?" I replied. "I thought it was obvious. It's sweet. I'm happy for him—he deserves someone nice like Quentin. I had no idea that Horace had such a sad life. He always seems so cheerful."

"Maybe there's hope for me yet." I couldn't tell if he was being serious or sarcastic, but before I could ask, he quickly changed the subject. "We should arrive in a couple of hours. What's the plan?"

"Get some information from Tanis, then talk to Uncle Pat. If John Berith *is* back, we might have to stick around for a while." I sat for a minute, watching the scenery go by, contemplating how to broach the next topic. Finally, I just blurted out, "Do you want to talk about what happened in Halifax?"

Gareth stared straight ahead at the road. "I should never have come at you in the way that I did. I promise I'll—"

"No," I interrupted. "I didn't mean that. We were both under a lot of stress and it's okay, honest. I was talking about what happened at the park. I was really worried about you."

Gareth chuckled. "Don't be. I'm old, remember?"

"Be serious," I chided him. "I told them we'd come back, finish the job, but I don't want the job to finish *you*.

You've always said the box is just a symbol—maybe *you're* the actual conduit. Remember what the woman said—'he is the one'?"

"I'm nothing special. And don't forget that I'd just run a four-minute mile trying to catch up to you. That's probably why I was so tired."

"Nothing special, huh?" I laughed. "Didn't the mere fact of your birth drive the floodwaters back?"

Gareth groaned. "I told you about that, didn't I? I was drunk if I recall correctly."

"Drunk or not, maybe there's something to it. Didn't you ever wonder why Julia died, but her spirit stayed with you? Maybe even as a child, you had some kind of power that John Berith is afraid of. And if he is, I'm glad—we need all the help we can get. But if crossing spirits over drains you—"

"I'll just do three or four at a time then," Gareth answered lightly. "We can make a holiday of it, stay a week or whatever it takes. But first, we have to get through the next few days."

We got to the village of Washington without any problems, stopping at a grocery store along the way to pick up some provisions. Mitchell was making good time from the London airport, so we drove to the next town, a little place called Drumbo, and had lunch at the local pub while we waited for him. He called just after noon to say he was pulling off the highway and would be at the Washington house in ten minutes. Gareth settled the bill while I freshened up. I tried to avoid mirrors at the best of times—I hadn't seen a hairdresser for months and wore my hair pulled back into a straggly ponytail most of the time. I felt sometimes like the road, and our work, was taking its toll on me, not just mentally but physically. Gareth kept joking about his age, but I looked perpetually tired, and older than my twenty-one years as well. Maybe when this was over, I'd treat myself to a spa day. I laughed at the thought and my reflection laughed back, as if to say, "Who are you kidding?" I sighed and went out to the truck where Gareth was waiting.

We drove up the road and as we approached the corner where the house sat, we noticed a small compact car waiting. Mitchell got out as we pulled up behind him, a smile creasing his face.

"It's good to see you," he said, putting his arm around my shoulder and shaking Gareth's hand. "I have to admit, I'm a little nervous. Excited, but nervous too."

I looked up at the house. The last time we were here, it seemed to be in flux, alternating between positive and negative energy. Now, it was completely dark—what I would have called a 'bad house' when I was younger. "Something's definitely changed," I told Gareth and Mitchell.

Gareth started to say something in reply but then the door to the house flew open. Tanis Gibson stomped out onto the porch. She didn't look happy. "It's about damned time! I need you to fix this, once and for all! I can't believe you just walked away and left that—that *thing* here!"

"Tell us what happened," I said calmly, hoping my demeanor would rub off on her. As I got closer to her, I realized that she had a deep gash on her cheek and bruising under one eye.

"Everything was fine for a while, then last week it started up again." She waved her hand vaguely towards the bathroom window on the upper story. "Every morning there was a new message on the mirror. One day it said, 'Beware'. The next it said, 'He's coming'. Two days ago, it said 'REDRUM' in huge capital letters. I mean, what the hell?! REDRUM—that's MURDER backwards! My husband thinks I'm out of my mind, that *I'm* the one doing it! And then yesterday, I was getting ready for work when all of a sudden, the medicine cabinet door flew open and clocked me in the face!"

Mitchell came forward. "We're very sorry this is happening to you. Allow us to go in and investigate."

"Who the hell are you?!" Tanis looked around at us wildly. "Another fake ghost hunter?"

"Tanis," I said sternly, trying to get her attention. "Have you noticed anything else, like voices in the baby monitor again, or anything near Kate's room?"

"No, but she's been acting strange. Every so often, she looks frightened and I don't know why. And the other night, I heard her talking—when I went in, she was awake and told me there was a 'black angel' on her ceiling!" Her eyes began to well up with tears. It was obvious that she was overwrought with worry and taking it out on us.

"Where's Kate right now?" I asked.

"Downstairs napping in the back room. It's too dangerous upstairs." She started to wipe her eyes and winced from the pain. "I thought I was going to need stitches," she sniffed.

"All right," Gareth said, shouldering his duffel bag. "We're going up to take a look around. I promise we'll be quiet and not wake the little girl. Stay with her—we'll come and get you if we need you."

Tanis nodded, resigned, and held the door open for us. As we made our way carefully up the stairs, I whispered to Mitchell, "Watch out. He likes to throw things."

When we got to the landing, we paused. It was littered with a variety of objects: a hairbrush, various items of make-up, two toothbrushes, a bottle of shampoo, and a cracked hand mirror. Mitchell whispered, "I see what you mean." We picked our way through the minefield of toiletries and as we got close to the bathroom door, I could hear bad-tempered muttering and cursing. I motioned to Gareth and Mitchell to stay back, and I peeked my head around the doorframe. Uncle Pat was standing in the middle of the room, arm pulled back, ready to jettison the curling iron he was holding out into the hall. When he saw me, he stopped—his arm fell to his side and the curling iron dropped to the ground with a metallic clang.

"It's about damned time!" he growled. He shoved his hands in his pockets angrily and leaned back against the bathroom vanity. "What does a ghost have to do to get a little attention from you people?"

"Take it easy," I urged him, stepping into the doorway. "We just found out this morning that you were back."

Gareth moved up behind me. Seeing the shimmer, he put a hand on my shoulder protectively. "You throw anything else and you're going in the box, like it or not," he warned.

"He's here too? Well, isn't that a treat. And who's the other fella?" Pat scowled, pointing to Mitchell.

"He's with us," I replied. "Never mind about that. What's the deal? Tanis said you've been terrorizing her, throwing things, writing messages on the mirror…REDRUM? I mean, come on."

Pat chuckled. "Yeah, I saw it in a movie once. Now *that* got her attention. Finally. Listen—you told me to let you know if John Berith was back. I don't have a lot of alternatives, being trapped in this particular area of the house as I am, so throwing her crap around and writing on the mirror is about all I can do. But he *is* back, and I needed to let you know. The bastard's been skulking around again. I caught him in the little girl's room last week and we had a 'conversation', and by that, I mean I told him what was what!"

"So you told him to get lost again. And how did he respond this time?" I asked.

"He laughed. Called me an 'ineffectual revenant', whatever that is, said I couldn't do anything to stop him. Said he needed the girl, that the one he had right now was too much trouble."

"Too much trouble?" I echoed. "What did he mean? Did he mention her by name? Did you see her?" I knew without a doubt it must be Harmony. I felt a flash of hope that she was using her strength against John Berith, that her spirit was still intact.

"No," Pat shook his head. "There was another presence, small but powerful, that's all I know. He kept her hidden, but it was obvious he was using a lot of effort to do it. He said, 'This one never ceases fighting me—her energy does not sustain me. I need rid of her.'" I told him if he wanted a real fight, he came to the right place. He laughed and said it *was* the right place, the veil here being so thin and all, whatever that means. When I said I'd never let him take little Kate, he laughed again, said something about 'his man couldn't be stopped', and then he vanished."

"Where did he go?" I asked. "Where can we find him?"

Pat scowled again. "You have a lot of questions, don't you? Last I saw 'his man', he was lurking in the woods down past the pond. Has a car parked in the old laneway hidden by brush—an ugly beige thing. You can just quite see it through the window if you know where to look."

The window was high up on the wall, but I stood on my tiptoes. "He's right," I said to Gareth and Mitchell after quickly summarizing what Uncle Pat had told me. "It's about 100 yards past the pond, through the trees there." I could see the sun glinting off the car's chrome trim.

"We should call the police," Mitchell urged, pacing the floor and gesturing angrily in the direction of the pond. "They could get him for...for attempted kidnapping!"

"With what proof?" Gareth asked. "The word of a cranky old phantom?"

"Who are you calling 'cranky', you sour-faced ghostbuster?" Pat was incensed and started looking around for something to lob at Gareth.

"Stop it!" I intervened. "Gareth's right. We don't have any proof. He could just say he pulled over to rest or use the bathroom or something. And if he's planning to get rid of 'the one' he has now, which has got to be Harmony, then we need to be careful, trap him before he can do that and I lose her spirit forever."

Mitchell stopped pacing. "Fine," he agreed. "No police for now. But I'm going down there to confront him — don't try to stop me!" With that, he turned and headed quickly down the stairs. Gareth picked up his bag and took off after him, calling out, "Mitchell, wait!"

I started to race after them when Pat yelled, "Stop!" I spun around — the look on his face was one I hadn't seen before. He looked heartsick. "I'll protect her until you tell me otherwise. But when all of this is done," he said dejectedly, "will you…will you come back with the box? I don't want to stay here anymore — it's just too lonely."

"Of course," I said gently. "I promise." With that, I took off down the stairs to find Gareth and Mitchell.

18

CLARICE'S VISION

When I got out to the porch, Tanis was standing there, a little blonde girl in her arms, looking bewildered. "What's going on?" she demanded.

"You won't have any more problems," I said breathlessly as I brushed past her and Kate. "Everything will be fine soon."

I got out to the driveway where Gareth was arguing with Mitchell, who obviously wanted to charge down the road without hesitation. "Be smart about this! We don't want to tip him off. Even though he's a super-malevolent, he's inhabiting a real man. The car is real too, and it has a real license plate. Let's get the number. Quentin's a retired cop—maybe he can run the plate and we get an address, hunt him down and find out what he's done with all the children he's stolen. Don't you want that, to lay Nicky to rest?"

Mitchell shook his head and rubbed his forehead with his fingers. "I can't stand it, being this close and not doing anything. But I hear what you're saying, and you're right. Better to track him and find out the truth, no matter how awful, than to lose him now."

"Good," Gareth said calmly. "Now here's what I'm thinking. The truck and trailer will attract too much attention. Let's get into your rental, cruise down to where that laneway starts. One of us can sneak up, take down the license number while he's busy watching the house."

"How can we be sure that he's still watching the house?" I asked.

Gareth looked at Tanis out of the corner of his eye. "Why don't you go back on the pretense of apologizing or something, get her to take you and the little girl closer to the pond? That'll keep him occupied."

I hated the idea of using Kate as bait, but there was no way John Berith would be so bold as to try anything with Tanis and me right there. Gareth and Mitchell crossed the road and went inside the trailer to wait while I walked back to the porch.

"I hope you're not going to hand me a bill after all of this," Tanis said defiantly. "I won't pay it!"

"No, of course not," I answered, strolling away from her, hoping to lead her down the path that meandered past a small barn on its way to the pond. "I wanted to explain, and apologize if there was any misunderstanding… my, what a beautiful pond you have…"

She put Kate down and walked on ahead of me, holding onto the little girl with her left hand and gesturing with the other. "Yes, but it's very deep. We can't take our eyes off this one for a second," she said, nodding at Kate. "You know, the other day I was hanging out laundry and suddenly I realized she'd wandered off and was almost at the edge of the water, chasing a rubber ball that she'd found, god knows from where. I've never run so fast in my life…."

As we passed the barn, I made a subtle gesture to Gareth and Mitchell. They emerged from the trailer, got into Mitchell's rental car, and started to drive slowly down the road. I looked straight ahead across the pond — it was murky among the trees, but when I saw a flash of yellow, I knew that we had somebody's attention.

I kept Tanis and Kate down by the water's edge for about ten minutes, chatting about our work. She accepted my apology and weak explanation that "sometimes they just come back". Remembering Uncle Pat's request, I added that we'd return in a couple of months for a "final cleansing, free of charge" and she seemed satisfied. Every so often, I'd look past the pond into the trees and feel Berith's eyes hungrily watching Kate as she toddled back and forth, chasing butterflies. I was barely able to restrain my rage. Suddenly I felt a strange sensation, as if I'd become the focus of something ugly and dark. It was reaching out to me with angry, dangerous tendrils, searching and questioning. I reached out too without thinking, giving free rein to my own fury and just as we were almost close enough to touch, I sensed shock and recognition, and the tendrils suddenly disappareted. A few minutes later, I heard Mitchell's car, the faint sound of its tires crunching on the gravel, and I told Tanis I had to go.

"Thanks," she said. "I appreciate what you've done. Sorry I was such a jerk about it."

"Think nothing of it," I smiled at her. I bent down and spoke to Kate quietly. "Be good and don't get too close to the pond." She stared at me with big blue eyes, eyes just like Harmony's. I felt a sudden surge of emotion, a mixture of grief and fear, and I walked away quickly towards the car before Tanis could see.

Mitchell was waiting in the driver's seat, waving a piece of paper triumphantly. "We got it! But something must have spooked him. As we were pulling away, he took off, heading in the other direction. I caught a glimpse of him as he jumped into the car — tan jacket, khaki pants, ordinary looking — just like always."

Gareth got out of the passenger side. "Let's regroup up the road in Drumbo at that pub where we had lunch. I could use a drink."

It was quiet in the pub. The owner, a friendly man with a slight limp, served up cold beers and went back into the kitchen to make some nachos for us. While he was gone, Gareth called Horace. "Is Quentin still there? We need a favour."

Quentin *was* still there, no surprise, and he quickly agreed to look into the license number. "I still have a lot of friends on the force who owe me. I'll call in a marker and get back to you as soon as possible."

Mitchell and I sat, drinking our beers and staring at our nachos, him drumming his fingers on the table and me tapping my foot, both of us too anxious to eat. Gareth was completely still, except for methodically eating one nacho after another until his plate was empty and he reached for mine. Finally, his phone rang, and he answered right away. He grabbed a napkin and whispered, "Give me a pen, quick!" He wrote something down, thanked Quentin, and hung up. Sitting back in his chair, he ran his fingers through his hair and then stared straight ahead, seeming distracted.

"What?" I prompted him. "Do we have an address?"

"Yes," he said, "but I don't know what to make of it. The plate belongs to someone named Samuel Bell, and the address is in Bruce County. It's in an area known as Little Egypt, bordering the Greenock Swamp, on the Egypt Side Road. Quentin did some digging—apparently the area is known as a ghost town full of abandoned buildings."

"Little Egypt?" I did a search on my phone. "This site says it was called Little Egypt because the head of local road maintenance in that area was a man named John Bell, known for being a brutal taskmaster, driving his workers like an Egyptian pharaoh until they dropped from exhaustion. Samuel Bell could be one of his descendants."

"Sounds about right," Mitchell said sardonically. "How far away is Little Egypt from here?"

"Not too far, actually," Gareth answered. "But we can't go there right away—"

"What?" Mitchell interrupted. "Why the hell not? Let's get this bastard before he knows we're coming!"

"Oh, I think he knows we're coming," I said, sighing. I told them what had happened down at the pond. "I'm fairly certain he's aware of us—or at least me. Sorry."

"Don't be sorry," Gareth said. "It would be pretty hard to sneak up on a malevolent like this one anyway. But we need to be prepared first. I have to get some supplies, and it's imperative that we come up with a solid plan. We can't just go in, guns blazing, and expect to defeat him. He's clever—he couldn't have lasted for hundreds of years if he wasn't—but I'm hoping that he's also as overconfident and narcissistic as every other malevolent we've encountered."

I checked my phone. "All right. There's a campground not far from the Greenock Swamp where we can get a site overnight. We'll get there and set up, then you take the truck into town to get whatever you think you might need, and Mitchell and I will try to come up with a few ideas."

Mitchell looked unhappy but he nodded brusquely in agreement. I went to the bar to pay our bill and the owner handed me the receipt and a small take-out box. "It looked like your dad really enjoyed the nachos, so I put a little extra in there for later." I laughed and thanked him. I didn't have the heart to tell him that I doubted 'my dad' had even tasted them.

The campground was called Aspen Heights, despite it being completely flat and surrounded by maple trees, but it had full shower facilities and a small laundromat, a real luxury for us. Gareth unhooked the fifth wheel and left for town in the truck. "I'll be back in a few hours," he said. "Then we can talk about the plan."

"What's he going to get?" Mitchell asked, as Gareth drove away.

I shifted the laundry basket I was holding from one hip to the other. "He won't say. He's worried that Berith will find out through my dreams. But I have no doubt that whatever it is, it'll work."

Mitchell grunted cynically. "I still think we should just go up there right away, not give him a chance to regroup. What if he's gone by the time we arrive?"

"Then we wait for him to come back. Look, I know delaying is hard, but Gareth and I have worked together for almost two years and I have complete trust in him. He has as much at stake here as you or me." I put the laundry basket on the ground and told Mitchell about Julia. When I was done, he sat down heavily on the picnic table and shook his head in sympathy.

"I would never have guessed," he said. "Poor guy. Do you think if he could do it again, knowing what he knows now, that he would have kept her, not crossed her over?"

"It's hard to say. Losing her the way he did—it's haunted him his whole life. He's dedicated everything to finding out what really happened to her. He's convinced that her death was his fault, that if he'd only told someone about his dreams, she'd still be alive."

"Seems like we all carry a burden of guilt," Mitchell said sadly.

I picked up the laundry basket. "I'd better get these things done. Gareth will be back soon, and together we can decide on the best course of action." I left Mitchell lost in thought, and headed across the campground to the laundromat. I sat for a while, soothed by the hum of the machines, watching the clothes swirl around and around in the water, trying not to worry about tomorrow. I didn't care what happened to me—my only goal was getting Harmony away from John Berith, and if I had to die to do it, I would, even though my own resolve terrified me.

I was standing at the picnic table folding the laundry when Gareth arrived back. He got out of the truck with two bags—one from a large home improvement and farm supplies store and another from a local antique market. I raised an eyebrow. "I can't believe you went antiquing without me."

He smiled grimly. "Next time," he said, and disappeared with his shopping bags into the trailer.

Mitchell had gone for a shower, and when he came back, we sat at the picnic table waiting for Gareth, picking away at the nachos the pub owner had given us. Finally Gareth joined us.

"I've been thinking, as I'm sure you both have. I think the best plan of attack is to go there, somehow force him out of the body he's inhabiting and then destroy him."

"With what?" Mitchell asked.

"Gareth's secret weapon, I assume," I answered. "But what about the children? What about Harmony?"

"Remember Mr. Wiggles? Once Berith is out of the body, hopefully this Samuel Bell will be able to tell us what he did with Melody and the other children. As for Harmony, that's where you come in. I'll need you to make contact with her, get her close enough to the box to pull her through before he knows what's happening."

"Cross her over? But why?! I need to talk to her first, spend some time with her…" I looked from Gareth to Mitchell, my eyes wide with panic. "You understand, don't you? If it was Nicky, wouldn't you want to talk to him, let him know you're sorry?"

Mitchell stared straight ahead and said nothing. Gareth put his hand on my arm gently. "There won't be time."

"You don't know that!" I shouted, pulling away. I got up and stood with my back to both of them, on the verge of tears. All along, I'd imagined that we would be reunited, that I'd have time with her, like little Jenny and Susan in Vancouver. Why couldn't she stay with me? Gareth should understand better than anyone—wasn't he wracked with guilt for accidentally crossing over Julia? But I knew better than to argue with him. Gareth was stubborn when he had his mind set on something, but I could be stubborn too—it was best that he didn't know my thoughts until we were in Greenock and I had Harmony. "Okay. Maybe you're right. It's getting late—I'm turning in."

Mitchell had decided to spend the night in his car with a blanket and extra pillow we had, so I left them at the picnic table talking to each other in low voices and got ready for bed. I feigned sleep when Gareth finally came in and settled himself.

I lay awake for a long time, full of anxiety but finally, around 3 am, I dropped off. Suddenly, I was standing at the edge of a forest, looking out over acres and acres of swampland. The air was humid; sweat was beading on my forehead and trickling down the side of my face. A bird called out in the distance, a mournful sound that echoed across the water. Something touched my hand and I jumped, looking down in fright. Big blue eyes stared back up at me. Harmony. My breath caught in my throat and I knelt in front of her tiny figure. As I wrapped my arms around her, I whispered, "Is it really you?"

"It's all of us," she whispered back. I pulled away and she pointed towards the swamp. The water was starting to bubble and swirl and as I stared, stricken, something began to emerge, something white and small and cold. It was a bone, floating on the water. I gasped in horror as another bobbed up, then another. More and more of them broke through the algae on the surface of the swamp until the entire vista became a terrible, watery graveyard. "Help me, Veevee," she said in her tiny voice.

I grabbed at her hand, but she was fading away, slowly disappearing. I called out, "I will! Don't go—stay with me!" I started crying and reached out to her as she vanished, the last of her voice carrying on the wind. "Veevee…"

I woke up, still weeping. I realized that Gareth was sitting up on the pullout sofa, wiping his eyes and sniffing. Our eyes locked. He said, "The swamp. She was there."

"I know," I answered, looking around for a tissue, the tears streaming down my face. "My beautiful Harmony."

"No," he said, putting his head in his hands. "In my dream, it was Julia."

There was a knock at the door. I jumped out of bed and opened it. Mitchell was standing there, holding back tears. "The swamp?" I asked, wiping my eyes.

"So many bones — just like Clarice's visions. And Nicky...."

We stayed up after that, talking until the sun started to rise, trying to shake our grief and get ready for the challenge ahead. "Eat up, everyone," said Gareth, grabbing the Fun Pak of cereal out of the cupboard. "We need to hit the road. This is what we've been waiting our whole lives for."

As I put the empty boxes in the garbage, I noticed the bags that Gareth brought back the day before, balled up and empty, and his duffel bag looked more packed than usual, with whatever he'd bought obviously in there. Well, if Gareth had a secret weapon, I could have secrets too. I was getting Harmony back, and no one was going to stop me.

19

BERITH THE ETERNAL

We drove at a mad pace, hoping there were no early morning radar traps on the road. Mitchell was following close behind us in the rental car—every time I looked in the sideview mirror, his face, serious and focused, stared back. It was only two hours to Little Egypt and we made it there in record time, the sun not even above the tree line yet. Gareth and I didn't speak much—we were both still caught up in the previous evening's nightmare. I kept seeing Harmony's sweet little face, and I knew that Gareth was haunted by Julia's. At least Gareth had had some closure—he'd been able to not only see his sister's body one last time before she was laid to rest, but he'd been able to spend time with her spirit before she passed on. And he had something tangible too. One night, we'd been out drinking, and he gave me his wallet to pay the tab. Tucked in among the bills was a folded-up piece of paper, yellow with age. I opened it when he wasn't looking and saw the childish scrawl of the words "I luv you mommy" and the stick figures below. He'd kept Julia's drawing all these years as a reminder of what? His guilt? His mission? At least he had that—all I had were memories. When I'd left home in the middle of the night over two years ago, after a last awful argument with my mother in which she once again accused me of having something to do with Harmony's disappearance, I'd taken nothing with me but the clothes I was wearing. My father, silent and complicit with her as always, tried to shove a ten-dollar bill in my hand as I walked out the door, but I threw it back at him in disgust and grabbed the car keys instead. I didn't know if I even cared to see either of them again, but if I did, it would be nice if their eyes weren't still filled with hate.

Gareth had the GPS on, and we found Egypt Line easily. According to Quentin, Samuel Bell lived down a long sideroad that ran between heavy forest and the edge of the swamp, in a cabin tucked into the bush. We'd already decided to walk in to avoid attracting attention, so we parked the vehicles, and all met behind the trailer.

"What we need to do," instructed Gareth, "is to somehow get the super-malevolent out of Samuel Bell's body. Then I can take action."

"Are you finally going to tell us what the secret weapon is?" Mitchell asked. "It might be important for us to know."

Gareth thought for a minute, then said, "We know that regular salt-and-vinegar hydrochloric acid works on your garden variety malevolent, but I needed something stronger. That's why I went to the antique market."

Mitchell and I both looked at him questioningly. He continued, "At the turn of the last century, a lot of homes and businesses were equipped with these round glass bottles full of a chemical called carbon tetrachloride. If you had a fire, you grabbed the bottle from its holder and threw it into the flames, smashing the glass and releasing the chemicals. In theory, it was supposed to put out the fire. They didn't work very well, so no one makes them anymore, but carbon tetrachloride is a really powerful solvent, and if it's exposed to heat, it creates phosphine gas as well. I found one of these fire grenades at the antique market, completely intact. Seems to me it'll serve the purpose."

Mitchell was concerned. "And you're what—going to just toss it at him?"

"Something like that," Gareth said. "I'm hoping that once we get the super-malevolent out of Samuel Bell, that smashing the grenade into it will…dissolve Berith, for want of a better word. We just need to make sure we're all well back when I throw it."

"What if Harmony's close by? Will it hurt her too?" I asked, alarmed.

"It might, but don't worry," he said, trying to be reassuring. "We just need to make sure we get her away from Berith first. And we will—trust me." Gareth shouldered his duffel bag and started walking. "Come on."

I put my doubts aside and followed behind him. Mitchell caught up and looked at me, brow furrowed. I shrugged as if to say, "What choice do we have?" and we set off down the quiet sideroad. The only noise was our shoes crunching on the gravel, and every once in a while, the mournful call of a bird in the distance.

"I know that sound," Mitchell said in a hushed voice. "I remember it from my dream."

"Me too," I murmured back. The sun was getting higher in the sky and the heat of the day was building, causing steam to rise off the waters of the swamp beside us. As we got further down the road, the air started to close in around us, creating a familiar vacuum of silence that warned of something otherworldly and dangerous. There was a laneway about 100 yards away, with a small marker at the entrance bearing the emergency number 4522912. I quickened my pace and pulled up beside Gareth. "That's it up there," I pointed. We continued on, peering through the trees to our right, making sure that no one was watching us.

When we got to the marker, we turned in. The laneway was quickly shrouded in shadows as the trees engulfed us. There was a bend up ahead, our path curving away into darkness. I felt like I was practically tiptoeing, trying not to make any sound that would alert Berith to our presence. I started trembling. Mitchell noticed—he wordlessly pulled up his shirt to reveal a knife in a sheath attached to his belt. My eyes went wide, but he put his finger to his lips. What was he planning? The sight of the knife didn't make me feel any better, any safer. As we approached the bend, Gareth stopped and held up his hand, signaling us to halt. I stopped, but as I did, I could feel that same awful sensation, those ugly, dark tendrils reaching out for me. I closed my eyes and held my breath, trying to stay unnoticed, but as they came close, there was a shudder of recognition and the tendrils recoiled. "Guys," I whispered. "I think—"

I barely got the words out when we heard the roar of an engine. A beige car came careening around the bend, aiming straight for Gareth at top speed. I looked around wildly for something I could use to try and stop it—there were rocks along the side of the laneway, and I grabbed the biggest one I could find. I ran forward and heaved it as hard as I could at the approaching car. The rock smashed into the windshield, shattering it. The car veered off, away from us, and headed towards the trees. Out of control, it slammed into a huge spruce with a resounding crash, the trunk of the tree practically cleaving the car's hood in two.

We all ran towards the wreck, Gareth in the lead. When he reached the driver's side door, he pulled it open. A man was in the driver's seat unconscious, his head nestled in the airbag, blood trickling down his face. "Quick," Gareth yelled. "We need to find Harmony!" I looked around frantically for any sign of her. "No, you have to concentrate. Focus your mind!"

I didn't know if I could, but I backed away to the other side of the laneway, leaned against a tree, closed my eyes, and reached out. *"Where are you? Harmony, it's me — I need to find you!"* There was nothing for a minute, and I was lost in the darkness. *"Harmony, where are you?!"* Then I felt something tug my hand. I opened my eyes and there she was, my beautiful girl, her big blue eyes locked with mine. "I have her!" I called to Gareth. "Come on, Harmony — we need to get back. It's dangerous!"

Her eyes were full of terror. "He says you're strong, but he's stronger," she whispered.

I grabbed her hand, pulling her down the road towards a cabin in the distance. "He's not today, my sweet girl," I said. "Stay with me." She reached up to touch my face. My heart leapt and I had to hold back my tears. I was never letting her go again, there was no question. But for now, there was the issue of Samuel Bell. Gareth and Mitchell were down the road — Gareth was trying to pull Bell out of the car but something strange was going on. Mitchell was advancing on them like an automaton, as though being propelled forward against his will. Suddenly, he reached under his shirt and pulled out his knife.

"Gareth!" I screamed, assuming that Mitchell was going to attack the man in the car. But as he got closer, I realized with horror that Mitchell was making his way to Gareth — the super-malevolent must have fled Samuel Bell's body when he was knocked out and found a new host in Mitchell.

"Stay here!" I said to Harmony. I hated leaving her, but Gareth needed me more. He turned at the sound of my voice and backed up against the car as Mitchell brought the blade down. Gareth side-stepped it as I came up behind them.

"Mitchell, stop! What are you doing?" I shrieked as he raised the blade again. He dropped his arm and twisted around to look at me. His expression was strange, distorted, as if it was Mitchell but not-Mitchell.

"The hunters must die," he intoned in a guttural, unfamiliar voice. Then his face twisted into a sneer. "You," he said. "I've been waiting." His face contorted again, and Mitchell's voice broke through. "Run, Verity!" he said hoarsely, then the sneering face returned.

Mitchell's arm began to rise again, the hand holding the knife shaking with exertion, a visible struggle as if a counterforce was attempting to pull it back down. "What's happening?" I yelled to Gareth.

"Berith has him! When Bell lost consciousness, Berith abandoned him and entered Mitchell!"

For a second, Mitchell's face was the familiar, kind man we knew, but it changed again, and he addressed us mockingly. "The two of you are pathetic. Did you really think you could defeat me? I've lived for centuries, watching empires crumble to dust while I laughed in their wake. I have been kings, warriors, the mightiest of the mighty and you have the audacity to challenge me, hunters?"

"Us? Pathetic?" Gareth scoffed, playing for time. "You steal children like a common thief. You're the pathetic one. Who is this man?" He pointed at Samuel Bell, still unconscious in the car. "He's no king, no gladiator, no *warrior*. He's just some weak vessel for you to inhabit. Is this what your powers have come to? How low you've fallen!"

Mitchell's face was furious, but his internal struggle was getting stronger. Just a little more distraction and maybe...I blurted out, "That's right. You're just a sad loser. Malphas the Profane was more menacing than you, and he was inhabiting a *cat*!"

The super-malevolent inside of Mitchell roared in fury. "How dare you!" it challenged us. Then suddenly Mitchell's face twisted again. Without warning, he flung his other arm into the air, the sleeve pulling back to reveal a multitude of scars, the physical manifestation of years of grief and self-loathing. With one last supreme effort, he freed the hand holding the knife and slashed it against his other wrist, opening the flesh and the veins beneath wide. He staggered, blood pouring down his arm, and held the knife up. "I'll do the other one," he said weakly. "My life for Nicky."

"No!" I cried. I could see Gareth out of the corner of my eye, reaching down towards the duffel bag and I knew what he was planning. Mitchell dropped to his knees, his head twisting back and forth as he tried to hold the super-malevolent within himself so that it couldn't escape. "Let Berith go, Mitchell!" I begged him. "Remember how much we love antiques!"

A glimmer of realization crossed Mitchell's face right before he slumped over. There was a moment of silence as Gareth and I watched, then a low rumble shook the ground, and something began to emerge from Mitchell's body. It stretched and grew until it was a pulsating mass of dark energy. Towering over us, it bellowed, "I am Berith The Eternal! I am more powerful than Death itself and I cannot be conquered!"

As the mass moved towards us, Gareth whispered, "It's too dangerous here. I'm going to draw it away."

I looked at him, stricken, but he turned to the super-malevolent and jeered. "You're nothing special. The world has passed you by. No one cares about you anymore." As he spoke, Gareth started walking backwards towards the cabin, leading Berith after him. "Come on," he goaded. "Let's see what you've got!"

He sprinted away as the super-malevolent became unhinged, charging after Gareth and growing larger until the mass of energy was looming over us all, blocking out the sun. The ground began smoking and patches of flame sprang up, licking the tree trunks and threatening to spread. The mass became a tower of roiling black clouds, encompassing the sky like a hurricane. Then as quickly as it grew, it abruptly began collapsing upon itself, dissipating into mist.

Gareth stopped, unsure, and then a small figure stepped out from within the dark fog that skirted the ground. It was a tiny girl, wearing a white dress, with a yellow bow in her hair. She held out a pale hand and spoke. "Gareth," she whispered, her cheeks icy and her eyes translucent. "The water is so cold. Why did you make me go into the box? I want to stay with you, Gareth. Don't make me go back to the cold water."

Gareth's eyes went wide with shock and he started to tremble. I thought at first that he was afraid, but no, it wasn't fear—it was a devasting grief that shook him to his core, and as he stared at the little girl, the sister that he had lost so many years ago, his entire body was wrenched by a sob that came deep from within him. He sank to his knees, oblivious to Mitchell, to me and Harmony, as he let out an unearthly howl that tore the air. I was terrified—without Mitchell *or* Gareth, I doubted that I was strong enough to defeat Berith on my own. As Gareth called out, "Julia!", his voice breaking with longing, I felt a tug on my arm and looked down. Harmony was staring up at me, her face angry and determined. She held out her hand, and suddenly a striped rubber ball materialized in her grasp.

"It's not real, Veevee," she said, gesturing towards the manifestation of Julia. "It's the bad man pretending." She pulled her arm back, then hesitated, looking at me for approval. I nodded quickly and she threw the ball as hard as she could towards Julia. It hit the ground and bounced up, striking the apparition in the shoulder. With that, the little girl turned, her face becoming menacing and cruel.

"You!" Julia roared in a voice much older and deeper than her appearance. "Always you defy me!" She began walking towards us, still furious, and with every step, the figure of Julia began to fade, transforming again into the monstrous cloud of energy. "I will destroy you! You will know no peace, no rest—you will live in torment for an eternity!"

Out of the corner of my eye, I saw Gareth shake his head, coming to his senses and beginning to rise. I knew I had one chance, one moment to give Gareth enough time to get out his secret weapon.

"Not this time!" I commanded, my rage matching Berith's. "Never again!"

The super-malevolent stopped at the sound of my voice and growled, "Human detritus!" The words thundered through the trees as it began reaching out towards us with its ugly tendrils. I moved in front of Harmony to shield her as Gareth quickly opened his duffel bag, pulled out the glass fire grenade and threw it as hard as he could into the midst of the undulating mass of evil that was John Berith. The grenade smashed against the ground, the chemicals inside it hitting a belt of flames, dispersing into the air around the super-malevolent and encompassing it. Gareth scrabbled backwards as Berith screamed and writhed, the toxic clouds of gas enveloping its form. It continued screeching as it dissipated, until finally, it gave one last gasp and disappeared. The only thing left was a black, charred spot on the ground in the shape of what I could only describe as a large, winged beast.

In the silence that followed, Gareth sat up, looking stunned, and I gasped with relief. Then we heard groaning and realized that Mitchell was on the ground, bleeding badly. "Quick," Gareth ordered, "call 911!"

When the ambulance and police arrived, they found me holding a makeshift tourniquet around Mitchell's arm, and Gareth guarding Samuel Bell, who had regained consciousness, but had no idea where he was.

"What the hell happened here?" demanded the first officer on the scene. "Can someone please explain what's going on?"

I relinquished my hold on Mitchell's arm as the paramedics took over. Harmony took my hand and smiled at me silently. Gareth stepped forward and spoke. "Call in a bigger team," he told the cop. "You're going to need to dredge that swamp."

20

MILES TO GO BEFORE I SLEEP

Gareth and I sat on the porch of the cabin, bone-weary, waiting to be released by the police. Mitchell had been taken by ambulance to the nearest hospital — the paramedics had replaced the tourniquet I'd fashioned out of a piece of my shirt with something more medically sound and assured us that he was going to be just fine. Right before they lifted him onto the stretcher, he whispered to me, "Is it over?" When I assured him that Berith was gone, once and for all, he smiled weakly and closed his eyes as if releasing a heavy burden from his heart.

  The story I provided to the police was a simple one: "We saw Samuel Bell lurking around the Washington property, watching a little girl. We followed him with the intention of confronting him, but before we had a chance, he tried to run us down, crashed his car, then attacked us with a knife. Mitchell was injured protecting Gareth and me, and then Gareth knocked Bell to the ground by the car, taking the knife and restraining him. When we found an assortment of children's toys, games, and a bottle of chloroform in the back seat of his car, we realized that we were right, that he must be some kind of predator. Bell was so overwrought at finally being caught that he confessed to abducting several children and drowning them in the swamp, so we called the police as well as an ambulance. Yes, officer, we know we should have called the police when we first saw him in Washington, but at least now you have the evidence you need to investigate further."

Gareth told them the same thing from his point of view, both of us hoping that the police were more concerned with finding out the truth about Samuel Bell than worrying about poking holes in our story. They'd taken Bell to the hospital as well, handcuffed to the rail of his stretcher. He was initially conscious, but when the police started asking him questions, he stared blankly at the officer who was trying to interrogate him, then suddenly began clawing at his eyes and shrieking in horror until he was hoarse—the paramedics had to sedate him before he blinded himself. Gareth and I speculated that, without Berith possessing his mind, the knowledge of the horrors he had perpetrated surfaced and it was simply too much for him to bear. I actually felt sorry for him, an unwilling slave to the super-malevolent's will, but with Berith gone, he was left to suffer the consequences alone.

I shifted in my chair to look at Harmony, who was sitting quietly on the floor at my feet, playing with an intricate origami unicorn that she said, "my friend Jenny gave me". Once Berith had been destroyed, she'd flown to me, wrapping her arms around me, and I felt her energy rush through me with blessed relief, knowing that her spirit was still intact. Thankfully, she had no real memory of what had happened to her. When I asked her, she said, "You were there at the bus stop, but then it wasn't you anymore. It was the bad man, and he made me go in his car. I started to yell for help like you always told me, but he put something over my mouth. I tried to fight him and it made him angry but I didn't care. I just wanted to see you again."

The police were almost finished searching the house, and we could tell by the flurry of activity that they'd found the evidence we were hoping they would, although some of it was confounding to them. Apparently, Bell had a box for each child that had been taken, carefully labelled and containing his "trophies", including Harmony's unicorn t-shirt and a pink bow that I knew from my dream belonged to Melody, but the dates on the boxes went back for decades. I overheard one officer saying to another, "There's no way our guy could be responsible for all of these — he's not old enough. But this place has been in his family for years. What are the odds that it's some kind of sick deviancy, passed down from father to son over generations? God, can you imagine?" Gareth and I could, but neither of us were going to tell the police what really happened. I wondered if there was a box labelled Nicky, and how Mitchell would react to it.

Finally, a sergeant came out of the house and told us we were free to go. Gareth picked up his bag and I held out my hand to Harmony. We all walked together up the laneway — when we passed the bend, we could see police divers in the swamp across the road. Based on Bell's "confession", they'd begun searching immediately. Little did they know what they would find, and I was glad to be far away when they started pulling up those small, white bones.

We turned down the road towards the trailer, and Gareth was silent. When we reached the truck, he turned suddenly and said, "We need to talk." He gestured subtly towards the little shimmer that he saw standing next to me. "You know about what."

"I don't care!" I said defiantly. "She's staying with me!" I turned my back on Gareth and led Harmony into the trailer. She stood by the door, looking sad. "It's okay," I said. "I won't let him take you away from me."

Her lip began to tremble, and her big eyes filled with tears. "But Veevee, I don't want to stay here. I want to go to the other place."

"What are you talking about? Why not? You'll be safe here, I promise!"

She came over and touched my face gently with her tiny hand, as tiny as it was on the day I lost her. "I know but my friends are there—Nicky and Melody. And I want to see Mommy. I can stay here for a little while, but Mommy needs me too."

"Mommy? What are you talking about? Is she—is Mom dead?" I was in shock. How could I not have known? Why wouldn't my father have tried to find me, to tell me?

Harmony nodded solemnly. "She's in the other place and she's so lonely. She misses you too—she said to tell you that she's sorry."

I shook my head in disbelief. "Harmony, how do you know that? Have you been to the other place? I don't understand."

She gave me a sad little smile. "I see things too, Veevee. Please let me go."

Just then, Gareth came in, looking uncertain. "Maybe—" he started, but the wistful expression on Harmony's face forced me to interrupt him.

"No," I said, the words ripping me apart. "You're right. But not here. I want to do it somewhere far away from here, somewhere peaceful." I turned to Harmony. "Do you remember the beach we used to go to, the one with the white sand and the high waves that we would jump over for hours? Let's go there."

Harmony nodded. Gareth looked in the direction of her shimmer and said, "You stay back here in the trailer, spend some time together. I'll drive."

It broke my heart that these would be our last hours together. We got underway, and I pulled out my laptop to show her Disneyland. "This is where we were going to go when you were older," I said. She laughed at Mickey and Goofy, her beautiful face shining with joy, and we took a ride on a virtual roller coaster that made her giggle with excitement. It wasn't as good as being there, but I would cherish these moments, knowing that I had as much to hold on to now, if not more, than Gareth.

Finally, we arrived at the beach. The sun was just starting to set. Gareth knocked on the trailer door. "You ready?" he asked gently.

I looked at him in anguish and said nothing. Harmony took my hand, and the three of us walked down towards the water. Gareth spread out a blanket and dropped his bag on it. "This is a nice spot," he said.

We all sat down, Harmony's face glowing in the light from the sunset as she looked out over the waves. "Do you want to hold the box with me?" he asked quietly. I couldn't speak, anguish filling my heart. He held the box out—I ran my hands over the symbols carved into the wood and then opened the lid.

"You're the best sister I could have asked for," I said, tears streaming down my face. "I love you *so* much."

Harmony wiped my tears away and stroked my cheek. "I love you too, Veevee," she smiled sweetly.

"Tell...tell Mommy I forgive her," I said, placing my hand on top of hers one last time.

"I will." Then she took her hand away from my cheek, put it in the box and disappeared.

I threw the box onto the blanket, and collapsed, sobbing hysterically. Gareth sat silently, his arm around my shoulder as I heaved and shook until I had no more tears left to shed. When I was done, he said, "I'm sorry. I've struggled with this every day of my life, ever since Julia... but it's the right thing to do. I didn't know any better back then—at least you had the chance to say goodbye."

"What if I never see her again?"

"You will. You just have to trust the universe."

"And my mother—I had no idea. I need to call my dad, find out what happened."

"You'll do that too. But not tonight. Tonight we'll just sit here and watch the water."

◆ ◆ ◆

I didn't call my father until a week later. By that time, the media had gotten wind of the story—The Swamp Killer was the headline in every newspaper, and stories about Samuel Bell and his family tradition of kidnapping and murder were the subject of every TV news show. Bell himself was providing no enlightenment—he'd sunken into a deep catatonic state, and his doctors believed he would never recover. Even if he did, according to all the pundits, he wouldn't be found competent enough to stand trial and would most likely spend the rest of his life in a mental institution.

Lucky for Gareth and me, we were mobile and could escape having reporters camping on our lawn—they never knew where we would be at any given time—but my phone rang ceaselessly for the first few days, everyone wanting an interview with the girl who refused to give up the search for her sister. I turned them all down, of course; that kind of notoriety would be bad for business. And I didn't want any fame, especially not for something like that. Mitchell had met with a couple of reporters from the more respectable news agencies, sharing his side of the story, which we'd carefully coached him on. He was a hero in everyone's eyes and rightly so, even if no one knew the truth but us—if he hadn't fought off Berith, potentially sacrificing himself to force the super-malevolent out in the open, we could never have gotten Harmony back or provided closure for all those other poor families.

Eventually, things started to settle down, and one night, I walked to the playground at the campsite in Port Burwell where we were staying for a couple of days, and nervously dialed my father's number. He answered on the second ring and said, "Hello." I didn't say anything for a moment and he repeated, "Hello?"

"Hi dad," I said hesitantly. "It's me." There was a long silence. "If you don't want to talk to me, that's fine. I was just calling to let you know I'm okay."

There was another long pause, then he said, "Thanks. I saw what happened on the news. Then the police came to tell me about Harmony and what had happened in Little Egypt."

Silence filled the line. Finally, I broke it. "Dad, why didn't you tell me about Mom?"

His voice was gruff. "I didn't know where you were."

"Yes, but you knew I had the car. You could have tried to track me down."

"I had other things on my mind. And I didn't think you cared."

"Dad!" I cried. "Of course, I—"

"I wouldn't blame you if you didn't," he interrupted. "We were awful to you. Maybe that's why I didn't reach out to you. I felt so guilty for letting things happen the way they did. We should never have blamed you." His voice broke—it sounded like he was crying. "Anyway, I'm sorry. And your mother was too—right before she passed…"

"I know, Dad," I said, trying not to cry myself. "It's all right."

He sighed long and deep. "Anyway, I was planning to have a memorial for Harmony next month, once all the hoopla has died down a bit and the reporters stop hounding me. I hope you—and your friend—can come."

"Absolutely," I assured him. "I have a few things to do first, then I'll be in touch."

"Where will you be?"

"Oh," I said, "We have to visit an old friend, then we're heading out to Halifax. We have some promises to keep." I heard Gareth walking up behind me.

"Sounds interesting," my dad said.

I turned to Gareth and smiled. "It always is."

21

THE DEVIL YOU KNOW

The hospital was quiet, lights dimmed. Only the faint beeping from a variety of machines along the corridor of the Chronic Care unit broke the silence.

Samuel Bell lay in bed, unmoving, hovering somewhere between oblivion and awareness. Whenever he came too close to the surface of memory, his mind would recoil and shut down again. On the thirteenth day of his long sleep, his thoughts rose once more. This time, however, before he could touch the edges of horror, he became aware of something, an acrid presence lurking in the forest of nightmares. If Samuel Bell's eyes, destroyed by his frantic clawing, hadn't been wrapped in thick bandages, he might have seen the small, hunched figure in the shadows of the corner of his room. Indeed, he might even have seen a flash of yellow from the other pair of eyes which studied him closely.

As he struggled against the tendrils of scrutiny weaving themselves into his thoughts, a voice spoke. It was dark and liquid and growling. It said, "I'm not finished with you yet."

Beneath the gauze covering his ruined eyes, Samuel Bell began to cry.